Reality Strikes My Dreams

Wayne Bien

Book design by Wayne Bien
Title page & chapter graphics except epilogue by Wayne Bien
Epilogue graphic by Ryder, Albert Pinkham The Race Track (Death on a Pale Horse). Cleveland Museum of Art
Poem "I Saw Your Face" Copyright © Wayne Bien 2007
Front cover photographs by Wayne Bien and Ryder, Albert Pinkham The Race Track (Death on a Pale Horse). Cleveland Museum of Art
Back cover photograph by Barbara Bien

Printed in the United States of America

First Printing

I Saw Your Face

Graveyard tombstones.
Losing their identity
to the wind and the rain.
                          You were there.

A nameless headstone,
                    long forgotten by relatives,
                          is a surrogate
for the one you never got.

I saw your face.
It shone in the sun
that crept through the trees
                    reflecting your image on the grass.

We talked,
just like before.
About how it was
and the things that never happened.
.
You have a place now.
A memorial,
                    on this Memorial Day.
                    I saw your face.

Acknowledgments

Tom Spanbauer though I have never met you your books and your "Dangerous Writing" approach certainly helped me find 'the sore place.' This book is the lie that tells the truth truer.

My writing professor Jade Gorman who took a student that thought he already knew how to write and taught him the principles this book couldn't have been written with out.

My editor and biggest supporter Barbara Bien who has spent many hours reading and re-reading manuscripts that in the beginning needed a lot of editing until we finally got to this one.

Chapter 1

It's September 1979; we had just celebrated Labor Day. I remember that because the races at the state fair ended on that day and I had gotten my trainer's license the month before. I was a groom for a trainer who had stalls at the fair so I just walked down to the steward's office one morning after I got my work done and told them I wanted to take the trainers test. They all sat behind gray metal desks in a room painted pea soup green with dirty beige carpet on the floor and looked at me kind of strange, cause they had never seen me before cause I was new, not new to the racetrack but new to going into the racing offices; never gone there cause I was afraid to talk to people, 'cause I stutter especially when I'm scared, and going into those offices scared me.

I didn't stutter that day though and I was proud of myself and I just looked at them right back until one of them told me about taking the test and how I had to see Charlie Phelps and pass the barn test first before they would give me the written one. I didn't see any problem with that cause I knew Charlie and knew I knew everything he was gonna ask me to do with any horse or saddle or bridle. So I walked right up to Charlie when I went back to the barn and told him what they told me to tell him about taking the barn test. He just smiled and said, "Come around here tomorrow after you get done your work and I'll give you the test."

So that's what I did, took Charlie's barn test, which was just putting some bandages on this horse of his and the bridle and racing saddle with the elastic girth and an overgirth. Now I'd never put a racing saddle on before because only trainers did that in the paddock before a race, but I had seen it done lots of times, since I was in the paddock too holding the horse. So I just put that saddle on over top of the pad and tightened up that elastic girth and overgirth like I had done it before and Charlie never knew the difference and passed me.

Took this slip of paper Charlie gave me saying I had passed the test down to the steward's office; they all stared at me from behind their desks. I handed the slip of paper saying I had passed to the guy who told me about taking the barn test. He was the oldest one of the stewards so I figured he was in charge. Plus he sat behind a sign on his desk that said Chief Steward, Albert Ferguson Esq.. I knew he had that Esq. behind his name because he was a lawyer and I guess because of that he was suppose to know the racing laws, which is what the written test is all about.

He, Albert Ferguson, Esq. looked up at me from the piece of paper saying that I passed. He has a reddened face. You know the kind you get when you've had too much to drink; he said in an aggravated authoritarian tone, "Be here tomorrow at 11am." The way he said it made me kind of angry. 'Cause I don't like it when people talk to me that way. I said "OK" anyway and walked out of their office with my shoulders all back and standing up straight to let them know I was all proud of myself again.

So that's exactly what I did: went to their office at 11am the next morning, took the written test about all the laws in horse racing.

I finished answering all the legal questions and filling out the diagrams about a horse's anatomy in about an hour. Albert Ferguson, Esq. had just stared at me when he handed me the test but I knew he wouldn't be there when I finished, 'cause the races started at 12:30, and since he was the steward he had to be there before the first race went off. So I just handed the test in to his secretary, a boring looking guy with a brown suit, white shirt, and thin brown tie, sitting behind one of those gray metal desk. Only his was older (you know, the army surplus kind). "Come back tomorrow around 11 and we'll have your score," he said in a voice that matched his looks.

I didn't feel so proud when I left there this time. I was worried-no-scared that I had done bad on the test and tomorrow when I went back for my score Albert Ferguson, Esq. would laugh at me and I would stutter when he asked me questions about my background and why I thought I would be able to pass his test.

I worried most of the night and kind of half ass did my work the next morning. My boss asked me what was wrong. I told him I had taken the trainer's test. He shook his head. The exercise boy and foreman Donald heard what I said and laughed and went and told the other groom Vicki, who was his girlfriend. Both of them looked at me, pointed their fingers and said, "Little faggot can't even rub a horse and wants to be a trainer. What a joke."

Little faggot. That's something I'll get into later. It's really what this story is about, about all the people like Donald and Vicki around the racetrack.

Eleven o'clock came around and I walked down to the steward's office. I felt like a death row inmate taking his last walk and the electric chair was waiting on the other side of the green steel door and its name was Albert Ferguson Esq. I could feel the electric waves bite me in the fingers when I turned the brushed aluminum knob and opened the door.

Reality Strikes My Dreams

Albert Ferguson Esq. and the other stewards and the boring secretary all stopped what they were doing and looked right at me. Albert Ferguson Esq. motioned me over to the chair alongside his desk. My hands began to shake and I was gritting my teeth. I sat down slowly awaiting the verdict. He opened the big desk drawer on the bottom right side. I could see all of the multicolored dividers. When he reached behind a red one and I thought for sure I was doomed. He held my test in his hands facing him so I couldn't see the score. A smirk came over his round face that was red again and made the blood veins surface. His blue eyes had a questioning look about them as he spoke.

"Mr. Brown. I didn't think you would come close to passing this test and I only let you take it because the rules say I have to."

The sweat started to pour from my underarms. I didn't know if it was 'cause I was scared or 'cause I just didn't like the way he talked to me; whatever, I was glad I had my long sleeve blue oxford cloth shirt on. It soaked up the droplets that would have fallen on Albert Ferguson Esq.'s desk if I had on short sleeves. He tossed the test face up on his desk, so I could see the numbers. But the sweat was rolling from my cap too, down my forehead and was burning my eyes.

I could see him look at me square in the face with that same smirk still on his face and say in a stern tone of voice, "You got the highest score anybody has ever achieved on their written test, a 98. But that still didn't mean you passed. Any smart kid like you could memorize a condition book. You had to have done as well on the barn test, not just gone through the motions, but really showed that you knew your stuff. So I checked with Charlie Phelps to see if he thought you'd be all right to train a racehorse."

The smirk changed to a frown and I thought for sure he was gonna flunk me.

"Seems he's stabled in the barn with you and told me about how conscientious you are and how the guy you work for keeps on promoting you and how the other grooms don't like you because of it. I hope that's the only reason they don't like you," he says as he gives me the once over.

"I guess I have to congratulate you Mr. Brown. You are now a trainer. I expect to see you in the winner's circle often." He nods his head towards his secretary, "He'll give you your license."

I shook Albert Ferguson Esq.'s hand just 'cause I thought it was polite to do so. I really didn't want to. There was something about him I didn't like.

I had to fill out some papers and pay my money to get my trainer's license. As soon as the boring secretary handed it to me I hung it on the tag that clips on the pocket of my blue oxford cloth shirt, right over top of the one that said "Groom."

So that brings us up to where we are right now: me a thoroughbred race horse trainer, and the three horses I train still stabled at the state fair after it had already closed and most of the other horses had already left to where the races had moved to.

Let me tell you about my horses, 'cause that's what this story is about too, horses and me training them and all the things that happened to me while I was training them.

OK, so after I get my license I need some horses to train, 'cause as I already told you, that's what horse trainers do. So my parents buy me this bug-eyed filly. I call her that (her real name is Lucinda's Pet) 'cause when she looks at you the whites in her eyes around the colored part get real big and make them look like her eyes would pop out; usually sign of a real nervous horse, which she is. We bought her from the guy I was working for 'cause even though he was one of the top trainers he could never win any races with her. Also, I was grooming her when I worked for him, and she and I got along real good.

Once I took over training her, I started galloping her myself in the morning. That was another thing Donald laughed about. The first day he saw me he pointed at me again just like before and started laughing so hard he was holding his gut and bent over. He stopped packing up (they were moving to the next meet) and walked up to the chain link fence that goes around the outside of the racetrack. He stood there smoking his cigarette and watched me go around the track.

The bug-eyed filly settled down for me and galloped real slow around the half-mile oval. I looked over at Donald when we went by. He looked down like he wasn't interested. When I was riding back (to my stalls) I had to go past where my old boss was stabled. Donald and my old boss were head to head and I heard Donald say, "He got her to go real slow."

Reality Strikes My Dreams

About a week or so after that I found a race in the condition book (the book that the racing secretary puts out that lists all the upcoming races) going a mile and a sixteenth instead of the six furlongs (three-quarters of a mile) she had been racing. I had thought it out being her groom and everything that the bug-eyed filly just wanted to go a distance of ground. She always went to the lead right out of the starting gate and then gave up when other horses came up along side her; but, in a distance race I figured she ought to have enough speed to get the lead all by herself.

So that's what I did. I entered her in that race. The entry clerk asked what jockey I wanted to ride the bug-eyed filly in the race. I didn't know any; so, I just gave him the name of one I remembered won a lot of races and hoped he would ride the bug-eyed filly for me.

You have to enter two days ahead of when the race is scheduled to run. So two days later there I was a racehorse trainer, getting ready to run a horse in my first race. I remembered what Mr. Albert Ferguson, Esq. had said. "I expect to see you in the winners circle, often." I hoped to see myself there too.

It was the first race that day and I met my parents at the track. I walked into the paddock to put the saddle on the bug-eyed filly. The paddock is indoors with glass all around it so the people can watch you put the saddle on. My parents were standing right there in front of me and the bug-eyed filly watching. I was proud of myself. I put the saddle and overgirth on just like I did when I took the trainers test from Charlie Phelps. The jockey I named when I entered the bug-eyed filly did end up riding her for me and I told him what I thought about what had happened in the past. He shook his head like he agreed, which gave me a boost of confidence. I gave him a leg up and felt my career was in his hands.

My parents and I walked outside through the big glass doors of the clubhouse. We stood just far enough up the asphalt incline that ran alongside the outside of the track so we could see the backstretch over the tote board that sat in the infield. A mile and a sixteenth race starts right in front of the grandstand and the horses go all the way around the mile oval.

The bug-eyed filly was real nervous before the start of the race. The jockey rubbed the side of her neck trying to calm her down as she spun around in a circle when the assistant starter grabbed hold of the bridle to lead her into the starting gate. I could see her weaving back and forth as the other horses were loaded. The back door closed on the last horse, the starter sprung the gate and they were off.

The bug-eyed filly leaped from the gate and had the lead before the horses reached the first turn. When they reached the backstretch her margin had increased to about five lengths; also, I could tell by the fact that the jockey was almost standing up on her that she was running easy and under no pressure from him. A quarter of a mile later the scenario was quite different. Another horse was catching up and the bug-eyed filly was being asked to run. Her jockey sat crouched close to her neck and with each stride she took he swung his left arm and then his right arm back and smacked her on the rump with his whip. Faster and faster he drove her with this pumping motion. The finish line was in sight as he glanced over his right shoulder to see how close the other horses were. His hard work paid off when he and the bug-eyed filly crossed the finish line first, two lengths in front of the other horses.

Reality Strikes My Dreams

My father was ecstatic counting the money he had won on his wagers and the forthcoming purse. He and my mother made many a patron angry as they pushed and blew smoke in their faces on their way to the edge of the track and the winners circle to have their picture taken with me, the jockey, and of course, the bug-eyed filly. I followed behind trying not to disturb any of those who had been shoved and damn near asphyxiated with their cigar and cigarette smoke.

And that's how it happened. The bug-eyed filly got the lead all by herself with no other horses looking her in the eye and kept on running and won. Funny thing about that race was my old boss had the favorite and ran second. I saw him and Donald after the race. "Never thought she'd go a distance of ground," was all he said and quickly turned away.

The best thing about that day was Albert Ferguson, Esq. After the race he himself, not the track announcer, said my name over the public address system, and that I had won this race with the first horse I ever entered. I guess he finally decided I knew what I was doing.

I got a big head following that; after all, I'm such a talented trainer.

But that's not reality.

I told you already that I was scared people might ask me questions, and as I told you I stutter and I'd get embarrassed; as a result of this being scared of people and answering any questions, I wore a blue long sleeve oxford cloth shirt, khaki pants, brown leather paddock boots that laced up the front with leather laces, and a British tweed cap everyday hoping those people I am scared of would think that I'm part of the horsey set, and too important to answer questions, but it didn't work.

Ends up the horsey set wanted to know where I came from, 'cause just like the stewards they had never seen me before, and asked me questions about that and I stuttered and got embarrassed and they laughed at me and knew I was made up, like a little kid whose wearing a hand me down Halloween mask that doesn't cover his face and everybody knows who he is.

That's the same way it was with the other racetrack people: the ones who drank hard, fucked habitually, had done some time, and came out smelling like roses. They could see past my costume easier than the horsey set did; in other words, they thought I was too soft and thin-skinned to be part of the hard edge environment of the racetrack and relate to them; still, they fascinated me.

I'd never been around anybody like them growing up as an overprotected kid, from a family who had no idea what life on the racetrack was all about. Don't get me wrong. They were good people, hard working, but everything revolved around the family store, making the almighty dollar, and they didn't know much about how to show their love for me, 'cause I guess no one had ever taught them. So, they bought me everything I wanted, which now was a couple of racehorses.

They, my parents I mean, thought this trainer thing was just another of my wild ideas that I would get tired of, but this was different; after all I had this love affair with horses, since the first time I climbed up on one, in summer camp, when I was five years old.

My parents sent me to college but I flunked out. It was boring compared to the job I had on a thoroughbred-breeding farm a good old boy auctioneer and his rich wife owned (her family has a bunch of car dealerships). These were the people I was now imitating with my standardized outfit.

Started to wear this getup when I was working for them; copied what I saw people wearing who came to see the horses. Cost me most of my first few paychecks to buy all those clothes. When they "promoted" me from the farm to working for their trainer at the track, I thought the outfit had something to do with it. But it just showed how naive I was.

Liked being a groom. Usually had three horses to take care of and take them to the races when they ran. Did my work and ignored any of the brash authority figures that showed up from time to time around the barn. Some of them were the owners. Some were racing officials; nevertheless, if they asked me anything, I always told them to talk to the trainer I was working for so I didn't have to deal with them. But now I was the trainer and had no idea what to do.

Like I said, Labor Day was just over and racing at the state fair had ended. The bug-eyed filly and two other horses I'm training are still stabled here. I wanted to stay 'cause it's close to where I live but the track was shutting down for the season. The racing circuit had moved not too far from here and I was hoping to get stalls there for my horses so I'd still be near home. Since I was the new guy I had to wait 'till the other trainers moved in and see if there was any room left.

This morning, when I pulled into the stable area, the guard at the gate handed me a note. It was from the racing secretary. It had been stapled closed so I tore it open to read it. *Harry Brown, you have been assigned stalls for the current meet at Tri-State Race Course. You must move your horses immediately.*

I got that sick feeling inside, where my heart feels all cold and I my stomach gets knots in it. Knew the racing secretary didn't like newcomers, but I thought since I had won my first race and Albert Ferguson, Esq. announced my name it would make a difference.

Wasn't used to not getting my own way and I wanted to pout, like I did with my parents, but who was gonna see it. Wanted to cry but that wouldn't work either. So it looked like me and the horses were moving to Tri-State, which would take me over an hour one way to get there; and I have to face a whole new group of these people who I felt uneasy around and captivated by at the same time, the predicament of my life, I thought.

But wait a minute I can't just give up. For the first time in my life I need to be proud of who I am. I can't be afraid anymore.

So instead of arranging to move my stable I decided to plead my case for stalls closer to home, with the one person at the racetrack I was most afraid of, Nick Costello, the racing secretary. I'd seen him around, and to me he was the demon I wanted to hide from the most but knew I never could. If you wanted stalls for your horses, he was the person you had to deal with. I had to give it a try and after I got my work done I drove to the races to see him.

Made sure I had my horsemen's parking permit and my I.D. badge, 'cause at the races the horseman park in the barn area and the guards at the gate were strict about you showing them your badge and parking permit. I had the parking permit hanging from my rear view mirror and when I got to the stable gate I flashed the guard my badge as I pulled in. He waved me on with no hassle so I pulled around and parked in front of one of the old red barns, not too far from the gray metal door that was the horseman's entrance to the grandstand.

Reality Strikes My Dreams

There's no sign on the door you have to know where to go 'cause they don't want just anybody trying to get into the races for free. But every year people figure it out and try anyway until they meet the guard just inside the door. He checks your badge again and throws people out everyday that don't have one.

At this track the racing secretaries office is in the grandstand behind the betting windows. When I walked to the glass door that said Racing Secretary I could see the assistants were busy getting entries for the next day of racing; I went in anyway. Told this nervous acting guy in wrinkled brown suit pants and a long sleeve white shirt with sleeves rolled up that had a brown tie loosened around the collar I just wanted to see Nick Costello. He just looked at me with his glasses half sliding down his nose and his eyes had this anxious look that made the creases in his brow in front of a receding brown hair line even more pronounced as he darted about the office without getting anything done.

"What's your name?" he said with a tone of voice like I was interfering with the panic he seemed to impose upon himself.

"Harry Brown," I said.

He disappeared into a room behind the main office and returned quickly and said, still with that disturbed attitude, "He's busy. You'll have to wait."

There wasn't a chair, so I just stood around and watched the activity. The nervous guy was just as abrupt with his co-workers as he had been with me. They all just seem to ignore his ranting, which made his fury even more intense. He let his arms fly when he expressed his frustration and flung the condition book listing the upcoming races he was trying to get entries for on the counter. His performance became more outrageous as time went on, with even more temper tantrums every time he would pick up the telephone and try to persuade a trainer to enter a horse in a race they hadn't planed on running in.

Well, this went on for almost an hour until I heard this gruff voice from the back room say, "J.P. send in the guy who is waiting to see me."

J.P., the nervous acting guy, came over to the door, opened it and let me in. I followed him down the hall where I had seen him go before.

J.P. stepped into Nick's office and said, "Here's the guy that was waiting to see you," as he quickly turned around, almost running into me in his haste to leave.

I stood there, thinking Nick would offer me a seat in one of the barrel back office chairs that stood perfectly lined up in front of his desk. Instead, his beady eyes just stared at me. With this smirk on his weather-beaten face and a mouth that held a cigarette he never touched. Just let it hang from his cracked lips so when he puffed he blew the smoke in my face humiliating me even more, as he leaned back in his chair.

Was real nervous when I introduced myself. "Mr. Costello I'm Harry Brown. I appreciate the stalls you gave me at Tri-State but it will take me over an hour to get there from where I live. Aren't there any stalls available here?"

The wrinkles on his face got deeper like his was thinking and I thought he saw my point. Then the smirk on his face got broader when he spoke in a comanding tone, making sure all of his assistants could hear.

"Who are you boy, that makes you think I can give you stalls here? The stalls you got are it."

He just stared at me again. I felt my chest tighten and I

couldn't get any more words out. I felt dejected. My father talked to me the same way. I turned around and walked back up the hall and heard him chuckle behind my back. His arrogance won this time, but at least I hadn't run from my fear. I felt proud of myself, even though I was facing a drive of 55 miles one way to work.

By the time I left the racing office entries for the next racing card had closed and J.P. sat at his desk leaning back in the gray swivel chair. In his hands was a copy of The Daily Racing Form that he held spread open in front of him.

"Thanks for your help," I said.

He looked up from what he was reading and with a sympathetic expression on his face said, "You're welcome."

It was a sincere "you're welcome" not just a polite one. Made me think he wasn't so bad after all.

Chapter 2

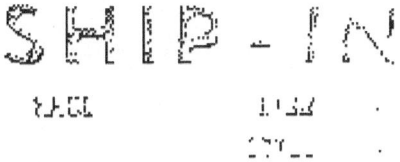

The following morning, temperatures approach ninety degrees as I drive my rusty, beige, 1970 GMC pick up south on Route 95; 30 minutes, 45 minutes, an hour, 90 minutes. The vinyl seat makes my back sweat and my underwear cling to my crotch. Warm, humid air coming through the open windows is little help in cooling me off. I keep a keen eye on the temperature gage hoping the engine doesn't overheat from carrying the load of hay, straw and feed in the bed. An overhead sign of grayish black with white letters reading Exit 10

Route 3 South is where I finally get off. Route 3 is a commercial area with every type of gas station and fast food restaurant along its path. After I drive about a mile I take a right hand turn at a street that makes you want to believe you are going into a housing development. This residential section of typical suburban style split levels and ranchers borders the racetrack. Once I drive past the houses the scenery changes to a depressing overgrown area with some rusty chain link fence on my left. The fence curves in and stops at a gravel road and there it is, the stable gate.

Turning left I pull up along side a grubby, little, brown shack with a tattered tarpaper roof and broken cedar shingles falling off the sides. The frayed screen door hangs open. The spring that had closed it is broken, rusted and dangling from its hook. A weather beaten white wooden door with broken windowpanes is closed behind it. Just beyond some more rusted chained link fence encloses the stable area and a corroded sign of faded red letters hangs on the gate. It reads:

ALL VECHICLES MUST STOP

ID REQUIRED FOR ENTRANCE.

Reality strikes my dream.

Chubby O'Connor stumbles out of the door, and defiantly stands in front of my truck. He is a short stocky man, heard he's an ex-jockey, although since I've been around the racetrack he's always been the stable manager of Tri-State. A beer gut hangs over his dirty khaki pants and expands his sweaty tee shirt to its limits. An NRA cap is pushed back on his head, exposing his receding red hair. "What you want, boy?" Chubby says.

I notice a shiny pistol inside a worn holster attached to his belt at his right hip.

Leaning out the driver's side window, I timidly say, "I was assigned stalls in barn B and want to get them ready for my horses."

"What's your name boy?" Chubby asks.

"Harry, Harry Brown."

Chubby's big hand with large fat fingers and nicotine stains waves me on. "You report back to me when you're done" Chubby shouts, as the open driver's side window of my truck moves toward him.

Worn holster, shiny pistol.

Reality Strikes My Dreams

Since barn B is located at the north end of the stable area and farthest away from the stable gate, my drive takes me past the numerous pole barns built after a fire destroyed all of the original ones in 1955, over one hundred horses died that night trapped in their portion of the blazing inferno. Two barns stand parallel to some woods. A tarnished sign with a washed out black letter B hangs from a pole on the far corner of the second structure; three empty stalls on the West Side are mine. The sun beating down on a tarpaper roof of the dilapidated wooden structure is making the 10x10 cubicles it houses very hot.

I parallel park my truck in front of the three stalls. My shirt and pants are plastered to my skin, as I turn my body to the left and get out of the truck, step up the asphalt curb, and walk across the dry, dusty dirt in front of the stalls. The first one has a broken hinge that has been tied together with bailing twine to hold it on the battered door. Holes in the floor are from a previous tenant's digging. The second stall is not that bad, but the third has a foot deep stench of old bedding mixed with horseshit and piss.

Reality Strikes My Dreams

Grumbling at the condition of the stalls, I pull the wheelbarrow, pitchfork and rake from my truck as the sweat rolls down my face. The complaining and cussing continues. Mucking out stall number three, the piss smell is so strong it burns my eyes, and the disgusting odor heightens with each layer removed. After an hour, it's finished.

My body's drenched in sweat; the uniform must be discarded. The British tweed cap, its sweatband soaked, is removed from my head where the hair is drenched with the sweat that now runs down my face making a brown streak as it washes away the dirt. The blue frayed oxford cloth shirt that covers the hair on my chest that is wet and flattened down by the perspiration is discarded.

I open the door and toss the cap and the shirt in the truck as I sit down on the vinyl seat that burns my ass with the heat it has absorbed. I quickly stand up and bend over, untying the laces on my paddock boots, which I toss in the truck along with the socks. But now the asphalt is burning my feet as bad as the seat did my butt. I sit back down. The seat has cooled off some. I look around, see no one and take off my khakis and underwear.

I sit completely nude, my body enjoying the cool freedom. I touch myself and wonder who else in the bunkhouse behind me is doing it too. My thoughts wander to a certain made up character and after the story's climax my mind returns to the work that needs to be done.

The holes in stall number one still need to be filled in; therefore, I need to find out where to get some dirt. I put my shirt, pants and boots back on and decide reluctantly to drive back to the stable gate. Chubby stands at the shabby white door of his office and looks out the cracked windowpane. He opens the door and yells, "You done boy?"

"No sir ", I say, pulling my truck up to where he stood. "I need dirt to fill in the holes in one of my stalls."

"You got a shovel, boy?" Chubby says.

"Yes sir."

"Well then, you better get your ass back to Barn B and go in the woods behind your stalls and dig you up some", he says, with a grin. "Remember I need to see you when you're done."

What does he want to see me about? Worry about what it

might be as I drive back to the barn.

As I walk back into the woods Chubby told me about, pushing the wheelbarrow that holds the shovel as its passenger, my resentments are growing for him and his smart-ass attitude. The bunkhouse I thought of earlier is on my way and sits to my right, across an asphalt road that runs in front of it. A young guy stands alone on the porch. He's medium height and slender build. His naked chest exposing smooth skin, tan from the summer sun. Shaggy blond hair hangs on his brow. His blue eyes meet mine.

"You the new guy who's moving in? "

"Yeah"

"What's your name?"

"Harry, what's yours? "

" Will," he says, and smiles at me.

Shooting pain in my heart.

The dirt in the woods is hard and full of clay. Thrusting the shovel into the ground causes it to kick back, removing only a small quantity of the soil, filling the wheelbarrow slowly, one small shovel full at a time and gives me plenty of time to take out my resentments on everybody associated with this dreadful place and the man who sent me here. It's a little cooler in the woods, but my body is burning up again by the time I am finished. I take off my shirt. My pants become dripping wet, as the sweat from my chest rolls down under the waistband, which makes a impression on the front of my pants outlining what's underneath.

Pushing the now cumbersome wheelbarrow full of dirt, I take the asphalt road in front of the bunkhouse, instead of the grass, on my way back to the barn. Will is still standing on the porch, and smiles as he looks at my naked chest and the front of my khakis.

Shooting pain in my heart.

The toil was worth it, as the dirt packs perfectly in the holes of stall number one. Using a bale and a half of straw creates a deep enough foundation in each of the three cubicles. Its golden wheat hue is a contrast to the dingy gray weathered wood that surrounds it.

Two screw eyes, one for each of the water buckets, are positioned on the wooden wall to the left of the stall door. Three more are needed in the corner for the feed tub. The thick canvas webbing that keeps the horse in its stall is secured by three screw eyes on each side of the doorframe. A single screw eye is placed on the top right hand side of the door. It will support a nylon net, which holds the hay. Each of the stalls is furnished this way in preparation for its occupant's arrival.

Ha! Moving back from the shed row, taking a look at my empire, what a fucking mess, three broken down stalls to match the three broken down horses that are going in them!

Reality strikes my dream.

I'm filthy, my chest is covered with dust and tiny pieces of straw which stuck to me rather than becoming part of the bedding. Locating my shirt, I put it back on, climb into the truck, and nervously drive back to the stable gate. "I'm finished

Chubby", I say, when entering his decrepit hovel. His large torso hangs over the seat of the grungy wooden chair he sits on, behind an aged gray metal desk. He looks me over with icicle blue eyes. A dirty holster and shiny pistol still hang on his right hip. Never seen a stable manager wear a gun. My eyes then notice the deputy sheriff's badge on the grubby white shirt draped over another wooden chair sitting on the right of his desk.

"You a faggot, boy?" Chubby asks, with a smirk on his face.

Shooting pain in my heart.

"No sir." I say, stuffing my true feeling of jumping over the desk and slapping his fat little face. The irritation must have shown on my face. He sensed something was going on and leaped up from his desk.

Worn holster shiny pistol.

"Don't you pop an attitude with me boy. I'll bust you in you little faggot face. We got too many around here now and the last thing I need is a smart ass queer. Don't let me see you with any, you hear? Now get the hell out and I hope for both our sakes, I won't see you in my office again."

Man let me tell you, Chubby is not the first person to think I was gay, and so what if I am. Brash authority figures, like Chubby, are people I've always hid from when the words gay, faggot, homosexual, etc., are mentioned. Until now...

Shooting pain in my heart.

Attended an all boys' school through the sixth grade. When I was in the first grade during the sixties we had air-raid drills and I remember one day right after athletics, we had just gotten out of the shower, and the siren went off. We all crouched down in the boys locker-room naked, facing the gray metal lockers and sitting on a wooden bench with varnish that made your wet ass slide off it.

I remember a boy in my class, Robert Kohn, sitting next to me on the bench, and as we faced the gray metal lockers our naked feet were touching and he slid his wet hip against mine. We were six years old and it was the first time another boy had made my little dick hard and I looked over at him, in between his legs, and his dick was hard too.

During the next five years I found several of my classmates attractive, talked about it openly, until I was told by an older cousin "Boys don't think other boys are cute."

Still didn't understand until junior high when boys start learning about homosexuality. Questions of my sexual orientation started then and so did my adverse reactions. Wanted to fight the first kid. A big mouth twelve year old named Alan Jacoby. I remember him standing in front of me in the locker room naked. Seems like after gym and a shower hormones begin to rage. Didn't have a speck of hair on his chest or around his dick. Just stood there shouting at me calling me homo cause I looked at his body. I grabbed the towel I had in front of me hiding my erection and smacked him with it. Seeing my physical condition he took off running to find the teacher.

I was dressed by the time Alan found the teacher who couldn't prove a thing and gave me one of those looks like I better watch out. So after that first time I just stuffed my hurt feelings and let them laugh. But the problems and my attraction for other boys never went away.

The next year another boy whose gym locker was next to mine asked me to "blow" him. I guess he must have noticed me looking at what was hanging between his legs every time he came back from taking a shower. I was already dressed one day and sitting on the bench putting my shoes on. The locker room was almost empty and I figured he must have already left. When I looked up from tying my shoes this naked body with a large erection stood right in front of my face. I wanted to do what he asked but there were still a couple of boys at the lockers behind us. So, I just shook my head no, got up from the bench and left.

When I reached high school I met Doug who became my best friend. I had such a crush on him. He lived up the street from me. We spent many summer evenings sleeping outside at my house or his. My raging hormones were evident each time we skinny-dipped in my pool. Doug just smiled. I spent many other evenings lying in bed fantasizing about more than a smile.

Reality Strikes My Dreams

Doug and I went our separate ways after high school. It's been years now and I still think about him sometimes at night when my hands are under the sheets. Now with Chubby's inquiry, questions of my sexual orientation have started again and so might my adverse reactions. Need to get back to the barn; the horses will be here soon.

The van driver is down shifting the eighteen-wheeler and applies the air brakes as he pulls up to the incline, built to unload horses from rigs such as his. He exits the cab and swings the heavy metal latch to open the side door of the trailer, and pulls the ramp out from its compartment so it covers the small gap left between the trailer's door and the concrete bulkhead of the dirt slope. My three charges are waiting to be released from their cramped quarters. One by one, I walk them to the barn.

All the subjects of my empire are now in their stalls. They seemed to have shipped to their new quarters without any problems, and wait for me to fill their water buckets and hay net.

In stall number one is the bug-eyed filly. A scrawny four-year-old with a meager white blaze on her narrow head and irregular white socks above her front hooves. I told you about her dark eyes that have white rims around the iris before. I give her hay and water first. She stands at the door weaving from side to side. Grabbing a mouthful of hay each time, she sways to the right. Her brown coat is covered with white sweaty lather. Winning her last race, as trivial as it was, makes her the star of the barn right now. Again, her name is Lucinda's Pet.

My next resident stands quietly. He has an air of class about him. His light brown coat shines and his warm brown eyes tell a story of races won and lost. He is older now and not as fast as he used to be. Under the front bandages his ankles are large and arthritic. He quietly enjoys the timothy hay. Captain Jack.

The third charge is a large bay gelding who bares his teeth and lunges at the door, with eyes that appear to pop out from his head and a scruffy mane, being tossed from one side of his neck to the other. His temperament is well known. Jockeys refuse to ride him and the pony girls cringe when they take him in the post parade. He's never won a race and probably never will. My parents bought him during a killer sale, keeping him from becoming dog food, and aptly named him Lucifer, even though his registered racing name is Rude Awakening.

My dynasty.

I stack the unused hay and straw at the end of the barn and notice that the new kid's act of moving in has attracted attention from the other residents of the bunkhouse. They hang over the black porch railings as if they were at a ballgame trying to catch a foul ball.

Recognize several of them from my days as a groom, some are pretty good horsemen. The others were the usual drunks and drug addicts. None of them were the "faggots" Chubby was talking about.

They have their own society in bunkhouse B. A groom named Reggie appears to be leading the populace. Worked with him several years ago, when he first came around the track. He did an adequate job, but it looks like the cocaine has changed him into an angry resentful young man. He looks much older then his age, around twenty-five. With a scowl on his face, his black skin is wrinkled and ashy. His bloodshot eyes have pupils dilated from the drugs. With nappy hair and a dirty white tee shirt and jeans, Reggie leads the uncanny group of misfits, drunks and hangers on, the guys who do a decent job but hang around just to pick up the scraps left by the others. Afraid to walk their own path, they follow their peers no matter how disastrous the outcome. The racetrack employs the unemployable. This group fits that testimonial. Except for Will.

He stands by himself on the other end of the porch. Why is he there not interacting at all with the others? Is he the gay one that the other guys make fun of? I know all too well how that feels. I wave at him, and as he walks down the steps, the others laugh and make kissing sounds, smacking their lips together, as he walks towards me.

Shooting pain in my heart.

Will walks with an ambling gait across the asphalt road, steps up the curb that's around the edge of the shed-row and comes over to where I'm standing. Still naked from the waist up his upper body is slender but the muscles in his arms, chest and abdomen are well defined. His shabby jeans are tight and reveal his bony hips and what appears to be the profile of what else he is packing beneath the front of them. The pants are just long enough to reach around the tops of his scuffed up brown boots

"You a rider", I ask?

"Bug boy, still got my ten pound allowance," he says.

(Let me explain, a "ten pound bug boy," or beginning apprentice jockey, carries ten fewer pounds than the weight assigned, until he/she wins five races.)

"I've got three horses to gallop in the morning", I say. "If you can give me a hand, maybe I can let you ride them in the afternoon".

His blue eyes light up and a big grin comes over his face. "You bet", he says and sticks out his hand for me to shake. It's strong, leathery, hard calluses on the palm, like the hand of a much older man.

"See you in the morning, "I say.

"Yeah", he replies.

Walking back around the corner to my stalls I hope that I'll have help in the morning. Getting three stalls mucked out, galloping the horses, cooling them out, brushing their coats, performing any therapy their legs may need; in other words, an exhausting routine for one person.

Approaching my stalls, I hear someone calling my name. It's Will, running to catch up to me. His boots clop, clop as the leather soles and heels hit the dry dusty shed-row. His jeans are sliding down the hips of his slender frame. I notice how white his skin is just below the waistline, where it hadn't been exposed to the sun. When he catches up to me, his breath wouldn't blow out a match; after all, galloping horses gets you fit. I watch as he pulls up his pants, "Can I take a look at you horses"? He says.

"Come on, it's feeding time and you can help me if you want". I say, eager to have the chance to get to know him better.

"There's something I forgot about when I agreed to help you in the morning", Will says. "I don't know if Mac will let me. He holds my contract and doesn't want me getting hurt on some other trainer's horse".

"Who is Mac?" I ask.

Will gets defensive. "He trains all of the other horses in this barn. Has some very wealthy clients.

"He was stabled in Florida last winter. I always wanted to work at the racetrack so when the racing came there (to Florida) last winter I ran away from my grandfather and all the his beatings.

"No matter what I did he had some reason to pull that leather belt off his pants and smack me with it until he raised welts on my skin. The last time I fought back. When he went to swing the belt back with his right arm I knocked him down with a left hook to his face. I pulled the belt out of his hand and started beating him with it. He managed to get up and got a couple of good punches in himself and bloodied my nose and gave me a black eye. But he never knocked me down. He's old and got tired quickly. The last time he tried to punch me I just pushed him away and he fell hitting his head on a table. I just left him like that, passed out on the floor. I knew he wasn't dead 'cause he was still breathing. I could see his stomach going up and down.

"When I went to the track they wouldn't let me in 'cause I didn't have a badge and wanted to call the cops because of all the blood on me and my black eye. Mac just happened to be at the stable gate, took one look at me, drove me straight to the hospital and paid for the doctors' look at my nose and eye. When we went back to the track he gave me a place to stay and got me a badge. Even helped me press charges against my grandfather, so he would leave me alone. When springtime came we moved up here and been here ever since.

"I've always been kind of small so Mac gave me the chance to ride. First it was just around the shed row, then I galloped some and now he thinks I can be a jockey".

Will takes a deep breath to calm himself, like he was getting ready to cry.

"Sorry", he says. "I get emotional when someone questions me about Mac".

"I understand. Sounds like a good guy to me," I reply.

The horses have seen us coming, and, by the clocks in their heads, know it's feeding time. Lucinda's Pet's weaving becomes more rapid. Her feet stomp, keeping time with her lurching shoulders. Captain Jack stands quietly and whinnies in anticipation. Rude Awakening charges the webbing. The screw eyes creak in their wood housing every time he throws his body against the canvas partition.

Don't have a tack room. All of my feed, hay, and straw have to stay in the shed row. The feed is housed in two metal trashcans, to protect it from the rats and mice. The first one is for the oats and the other the sweet feed, I also have a chain, which runs through the handles on the sides and lid of the cans locking back onto itself. This protects it from the two-legged varmints. The hay and straw are stacked on the wall at the end of the barn. Protected from the rain but not from anyone who finds it to their liking.

Each horse has its own white five-gallon bucket that I make up their feed in. Handing the first white bucket of oats, mixed with the sticky, molasses coated sweet feed of mixed grains and vitamins, to Will, I say "take it to the first stall", as I tell him about each horse.

"That's Lucinda's Pet." He watches her weaving dance behind the webbing and waits for her to lean to the right, unhooks the bottom snap on the left hand side of the stall door, which allows him to bend down, go under it, and put the feed in its tub.

"Is she always this fractious?" he asks.

"Sometimes worse", I say. "She will test you in the morning. Once you get her to the track, after her wheeling and ducking at everything she sees, she will try to run off with you. However, she did win her last race," I say with a smile. Will doesn't seem impressed.

I get the next ration ready, walk to the second stall, unhook the webbing, stoop under it and give it to Captain Jack. "This is my best horse", I tell Will, as I come out of the stall. "His name is Captain Jack. You might have heard of him".

"Yeah," he says, "I think I've seen him run. He walks out of the starting gate, falls back to last, starts running the last three eighths of the race, and catches them at the wire".

"That's him", I say. "He's won twenty five races running like that. He's a pleasure to gallop, when he goes to the track, which isn't too often".

"How come?" Will asks.

"Bad ankles and suspensory," I say. "He's made over three hundred starts in the last eight years, and they have taken their toll. He spends most mornings walking around the shed row and in the whirlpool. I only run him about once a month, if that. He doesn't need a lot of training. Been in the money, over half the times he's started. I think he knows his way around the oval," I say, jokingly.

"Who's the horse in the last stall?" Will asks.

"Rude Awaking, sometimes known as Lucifer. Haven't you heard about him in the jock's room?"

Will wrinkles his brow, as he is thinking. "Is he the one you can't saddle in the paddock and savages the pony in the post parade?"

"Yeah", I answer, not proud of my horse's bad reputation. "He's not as bad as it seems, just funny about his head," I explain. "Story goes he gave the previous trainer a hard time when they broke him. So they tied him up, blindfolded him, and hit him between the ears any time he reared up. Because of that, he's on the defensive anytime someone approaches."

I walk over with the feed. Rude Awaking lunges at the door as if to bite me. I stand there and talk to him quietly. He stops his aggressive behavior and lets me in the stall. I dump the feed in his tub and leave.

"He's starting to trust me," I tell Will.

"Don't worry about any bad behavior in the mornings. I will walk you to the track if you get a chance to ride him," I say. "He gallops good, he's just so big and gangly it's going to take him awhile to get his act together."

"I'll ask Mac", Will says. "As a ten pound bug boy, I need all the mounts I can get".

"What's up with the guy at the stable gate?" I ask Will.

"You talking about Chubby O'Connor?" he replies.

"Yeah, wanted to know if I was a faggot. Told me when I first came in that he had to see me when I was finished setting up my stalls. Went back up there right before the horses got here and that's what he wanted to know."

"He asked every guy around here that. He doesn't like queers", Will tells me. "He'll be watching you even closer after he sees you with me".

"Why's that?" I ask.

"A rumor, and lets just leave it at that for now," Will says. He hangs his head and seems so sad. His reaction reminds me of how I feel when guys would tease me about being gay.

I tell Will, "OK, no more questions asked. But I'm here if you ever want to talk about it."

"Maybe some day," Will says. "See you in the morning", as

he walks with his head still hanging down back to the bunkhouse.

"See you then ", I reply.

Getting into my truck to leave, I take another look at my empire. As meager as it is, I hope it's all here in the morning.

Reality strikes my dream.

Start the old GMC up. The truck has been sitting in the blazing sun for several hours, so the inside is even hotter then before. The steering wheel is scorching to the touch and the vinyl seat is again burning my legs and ass through my pants. I get out and keep both of the doors open for a while until it cools down inside. Driving out of the stable area Chubby is standing at the gate. I hope he doesn't stop me. He just glares, as if he knows who I have been talking to. I stop the truck by the Pepsi machine that sits by itself on the right hand side of the stable gate, and get a soda for the ride home. I can feel Chubby's eyes piercing the skin on my back. I keep my head lowered as I walk back to the truck, so as not to meet his defiant stare.

Worn holster, shiny pistol.

Driving out the stable gate the six-cylinder engine runs effortlessly. The load is much lighter now that I have unloaded the hay, straw and feed.

Past rusty chain link fence, through the housing development, by the gas stations and fast food joints, I approach the entrance ramp for exit 10; increase my speed and the air that drifts in the windows gets cooler.

Open the Pepsi, take the first swig and put it in the cup holder hanging from the driver's side window. The inside of the truck is still very hot. Hold the steering wheel with one hand and use the other to pull my shirttail out from under my khakis, and unbutton each of the front buttons. Pull the left-hand side back so the shoulder strap of the seat belt holds it open and tuck the right side under my right arm. The fresh air clashing with my sweaty chest hair is refreshing.

My sweaty underpants lie on the floor of the truck. Thank God they aren't clinging to my crotch anymore. Undo the belt of my pants and pull the zipper down, hoping this little bit of nudity will keep my head clear for the long drive home.

Take a drink of the Pepsi.

Thoughts of Will keep my mind occupied during the initial portion of the lengthy drive. Is Mac going to let him help me? Is tomorrow going to be strictly business, or are those innocent looking blue eyes and boyish grin tell tale signs of other intentions. Don't have to put him on my horses when they race in the afternoon if he can't ride.

It might be easier said than done. Have always let people's emotions influence how things are reasoned out, especially if those emotions have anything to do with gay, faggot, homosexual, etc.

Shooting pain in my heart.

For example let me tell you about Steve. He was a hot walker for another trainer in the same barn where I worked as a groom. He used to have a lot of trouble walking horses. I helped him out one time when a horse he was walking got spooked and he turned it loose and fell down. His gaydar must have been working 'cause after that he used to take his shirt off when he was finished walking the last horse and sit on a bale of straw outside of a stall where I was finishing up putting bandages on a horse. Placing his arms behind him, he pushed his chest and pelvis out in a suggestive pose that not only made his skinny upper body accent his soft white skin but also outlined the bulge in the front of his pants.

His boss was a drunk and made fun of him calling him a skinny faggot anytime he could. Steve would never respond; instead, he let the verbal abuse continue along with the tears he shed as he walked with his head down around the barn. He used to raise his head and look at me when he walked by. He was so cute and I felt for him. I wanted to hug him and wipe away his tears and tell him I understood.

But that's not reality.

One morning around 10 o'clock Steve had finished his work and was walking up the shed row on his way to the track kitchen. His boss staggered along side of him continually calling him a faggot. I had had enough. When they got to where I was standing I walked out into the shed and stood nose to nose with the trainer and called him a drunken bastard. My boss was standing just up the shed row and fired me on the spot. Steve's boss loved it. "What you gonna do now you skinny faggot?" Steve kicked him in the shin and his boss fired him too.

The word spread quick that I was a faggot lover. That's right a faggot lover who took the so-called faggot home with him that day. After getting fired I decided to keep my mouth shut through it all. All things considered it seemed to be a better solution to me than another Alan Jacoby.

After we both got fired Steve didn't understand what was going on when I took his hand as we walked out of the stable area. "You need a ride?" I asked. We both climbed in my truck. When we started out of the parking lot gate he began to give me directions to where he lived.

"Don't bother," I told him. "You're going home with me if you want to." He agreed, slid over on the vinyl seat and put his head on my shoulder as he cried uncontrollably. I put my hand on his leg and that's the way we drove through the city. When we made the left hand turn on to the highway my hand made a change in direction too and moved north and came to rest on what expanded the front of his jeans. My khaki's had a wet spot in the front where my swollen flesh was leaking. Steve never noticed as he was burying his face in my armpit wiping his tears on my oxford cloth shirt. My apartment was another 15 minutes away and my raging hormones couldn't get there soon enough.

Shooting pain in my heart.

We got undressed as soon as we got there. Believed we were just fucking to see what it was like. I found out I liked it a lot and let him stay. He was the first guy I ever wanted to live with. We slept together that night in the nude, our hands exploring each other's bodies; however, in the morning he was gone. He stole my Minolta 35mm camera as well as my virginity. I realized then he just wanted a place to sleep and someone to screw and in my mind I threw his ass out but he wasn't gone.

As I said I got both of us fired so I needed to find another job. I didn't dare tell my parents even though it was just a matter of time before they found out. They came to the track every morning. After all, it was their trainer I was working for. It was their horses I was grooming.

Had a girlfriend, when I first met Steve. Have been attracted to individuals of both sexes; nonetheless, I never fucked her or any other girl, never been past second base.

Reality strikes my dreams.

I take a drink of the Pepsi.

That's enough about Will and my twisted relationships. I'm about half way home and get ready to pay the toll for the Harbor Tunnel. Zip my pants back up. It's 7PM and most of the rush hour traffic has gone through the tube. The toll clerk tears the commuter ticket out of the voucher book that I hand her. Get the green light, and the barrier goes up, like a penis going from half-staff to full erection.

Shooting pain in my heart.

Drive north on Route 95 and develop a plan for getting all of my work done in the morning.

It's good that I can drive my truck into the stable area, my tack room on wheels. Keep the pitchfork, rake, shovel and wheelbarrow in the truck bed. My tack and all of the brushes, bandages, liniments and the other equipment I will need to take care of the horses, can stay on the passenger's side of the front bench seat.

Number the chores in my mind.

1. Arrive at the barn and feed the horses breakfast.

2. Run my hand down each of my horse's legs, to check for any heat or swelling, especially Captain Jack. His old ankles and suspensories that run on both sides of his legs from the knee to the ankles need constant care. He has to get in the whirlpool almost every day for an hour and his front legs get at least a rub down with Beageloil and bandaged. Sometimes the heat in his legs requires a clay poultice to draw out the inflammation.

3. Muck out their stalls. It's not my favorite job, but picking up the shit and piss everyday keeps the little 10x10 house from getting like number three was when I first got here.

4. Walk Captain Jack around the barn for twenty minutes,

and leave him in the whirlpool, while I get the others horses out to exercise.

5. Find a hot walker, so I can get the horses out to the track and back without having to stop and walk each one before I go on to the next. It's always hard to find anyone but a drunk or a green kid to walk a horse for $2.00. But that's all they get. Started out like that, and just kept hanging around until I got a chance to groom, gallop and finally learn enough to get my trainer's license.

6. Lucinda's Pet is first to the track, if Will is able to help me great. If not I can gallop Lucinda's Pet and Rude Awaking. I've been doing it so far, and my weight of 150 pounds is not considered too heavy.

7. If I don't have any help I will do it all myself. Its not impossible, just very tiring.

Reality strikes my dream.

That's enough planning; I am getting off Route 95 and will be home in five minutes.

Reality Strikes My Dreams

I finish the last of my Pepsi.

Chapter 3

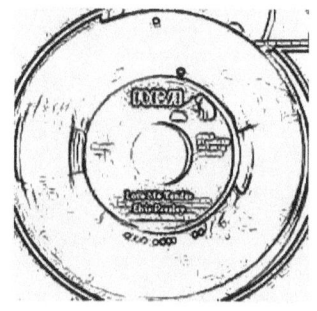

Making the right hand turn into the lane of my farm I am met by my zany Welsh Corgi, Chester. He chases the truck up the hill of the winding path, his short legs moving very fast to keep up. Should have known something wasn't right when his breeders gave him to me for free. The story goes that the people, who originally bought him for $500.00, brought him back without asking for a refund, just so he would stop running away and terrorizing their prestigious Baltimore neighborhood.

Reality Strikes My Dreams

He welcomes me as I get out of my truck, jumping up on the leg of my khakis. His brown eyes glisten and his tongue hangs down from his tapered snout, as he pants from his long run. As I reach down to pet his thick russet and white coat he darts away, always wanting to keep a safe distance from me.

Being outside all of the time, on the farm, has helped this senseless behavior of his to the point where he wants some contact with humans. When I first brought him here, he took off running, and would keep a close lookout, never letting anyone get close. I would feed him out in the barn with the horses and see him disappear in there only when he was sure there was no one around.

I told you earlier my parents bought me the three horses I train to help me get started.

But that's not reality

They bought racehorses, about ten years ago, and gave them to a prominent trainer. The one I told you I got fired from because of Steve. You see before when I was in college and even before that, I worked in the family business, because that's where my father wanted me to work, even though I never liked it. The job on the breeding farm was part time, my day off from the store and on Sundays. When the people who owned the farm sent me to the racetrack I finally quit working for my parents and went to the racetrack full time. After awhile they saw I was serious and when I got my trainer's license, they bought Lucinda's Pet. They already had Lucifer. I think their old trainer was glad to get rid of him. Then right after the bug-eyed filly won, I talked them into Captain Jack.

You see. I just got this farm from them 'cause they're getting old and can't keep it up. When they decided to move out they told me they were leaving it to me anyway so I might as well move in now. They still officially own it but they leave me alone and let me do what I want to the place. They didn't do any repair to the farm and left everything just the way it was for the last four years. Eventually, this farm and all three of these horses will belong to me and run as owned and trained by Harry Brown.

The farm is only five acres. My parents bought the land and had the house and barn built, to have a place to keep their broodmares. That's how they first got started with the horses, broodmares. Thought it would be cheaper to breed their own and it looked that way in the beginning. First horse they bred was a stakes winner, but it was all downhill from there.

After the next two foals never won a race they started buying horses already in training, either at auctions or through the claiming box.

Let me explain: an owner can claim or purchase a horse, out of a calming race for the price it is running for. You don't get to examine the horse before you put up your money. The purchase is based on the horse's past racing performances and any information that might have been gathered from watching their previous races. The greater majority of races run are of this type.

All of my horses run for claiming tags, anywhere from three thousand to five thousand dollars. That's how we got Captain Jack.

His previous trainer was running him for a three thousand dollar tag, thinking no one would claim him, because of his bad ankles and the fact that he was ten years old. The horse had won twenty-two races by then, and was in the money most of the time, so like I said after the bug-eyed filly won my parents took a chance and claimed him. I think it was the best purchase they ever made.

Anyway, the farm has a three-stall pole barn and about three acres of fenced pasture. Have two retired racehorses that live here. They were mine before I got this place, and right now they're standing out in the field eating grass.

The old gelding is my pet. Another hard knocking racehorse, he broke down in his last race, on a sloppy track that was thawing out from a winter night's freeze. Running in those terrible conditions, he bowed the tendon that runs behind and between his knee and ankle, in his left front leg. The tendon came loose from its sheath and needed a year to heal. I was his groom, and ran out on the track, after it happened, helping him into the horse ambulance that took us back to the barn. The owners didn't want to spend the time or money his recovery was going to take, so they gave him to me. Diamond Dan.

Spent the next year hosing Dan's, leg and putting a poultice on it, to draw out the heat and inflammation. He and I took walks everyday. In the beginning, it was just outside to the hose. Eventually, I would spend an hour walking him around the farm, as he munched grass and Chester barked at him. Welsh Corgis are herding dogs; I think Chester thought he was helping me get Dan back to the barn.

He still barks at Dan in the field, and Dan playfully runs after him. They have become buddies. Whenever I can't find Chester, the first place I look is out in the pasture or, if the horses are in their stalls, I can usually find him sleeping in front of Dan's.

After the year was up, I started riding Dan. His old leg got so good that the pleasure rides became exercise. We galloped everyday, over the rolling hills, around the farm. We both became very fit. Didn't want to run him again at the racetrack, so I entered him in a flat race that was part of a local steeplechase meet, that spring.

This was my first and only time riding a horse in a race. We both had fun. Dan tried very hard and finished fourth in a field of twelve. A few days later his tendon was carrying some heat so I retired him once and for all.

After that race, while I was walking Dan to cool him out, a very attractive woman wandered over to the area behind the horse van. Her long blond hair glistened in the sun. She was dressed in a long sleeve white blouse, the top two buttons open, exposing her cleavage. The shirttails were pulled out, over a pair of jeans that snugly fit her slender hips and legs. Her face and the exposed area of her chest are very tan for this early in the spring.

She struck up a conversation. "I thought your horse ran well."

"Thank you," I said, admiring her blond hair and as she bends over in front of me to pick a four-leaf clover, her blouse balloons open. I notice she isn't wearing a bra and I could see her breasts all the way down to the nipples. Everything else about her had dollar signs written all over it. The crisp white blouse, the new designer jeans, and the polished paddock boots, all spoke of new money. Different from the way Mr. Albert Ferguson, Esq. and his wife probably look. Expensive clothes but well worn from many hours at Alex Brown, the law office, the garden club, afternoon teas, or duties as chief steward for the Racing Commission.

"He tries very hard every time he runs. This was his first race in over a year," and I tell her Dan's saga.

"What a wonderful story, I wish more old racehorses ended up like this," she said. "By the way my name is Mary, Mary Strabowski."

"Are you a rider?"

"Never thought you were going to ask," Mary responds. "I am riding in the last race today. Same course you rode but it's over hurdles. It's only two races from now. Are you going to stay and watch?"

Thinking out loud I say, "I don't want to put Dan in the van by himself but he is so quiet... I can walk him over closer to the races. Sure, I'll stay and watch."

"Hope to see you after the race," she says; then, she smiles, turns around and walks back up the gently rolling hill. The breeze catches her shirttail and it flaps exposing the tight jeans covering her well-formed ass.

Dan continued to munch grass as we walked around the area the vans were parked in. He was so well behaved. Nothing like the nasty individual who wheeled around and tried to kick me when he was stabled at the racetrack.

I was scared of Dan when I first started grooming him. He bit me on the way to the barn the day the owners claimed him. And when I got him back to his stall he performed his first wheel and kick routine, his back hoof just missing my head. After a few times I realized that he had perfect aim with those aluminum shoes and was purposely missing me just as a warning not to abuse him like he had evidently experienced before. I respected him for that and after awhile he started to trust me and gave up on the wheel and kick.

But anytime a vet or anyone besides me wanted to get into his stall the old behavior came back to life and I had to go into the stall first, hold his head and reassure him that everything was all right.

The day he broke down, I cried and was so visibly upset that the vet wanted to give me some sedative along with the horse. Once the owners decided to give him to me instead of putting him down, which is what happens to most old geldings, I was able to get myself under control and began the long process of bringing Dan back to health.

By the time Mary's race came around Dan was completely cooled out so he and I walked up towards the course. Dan picked his head up, pricked both of his ears and tilted his head as if to listen when the voice on the public address system announced, "And they're off." We stood right there, Dan listening and me watching Mary's race.

Mary got the lead as soon as the race began. Since there had been two other hurdle races that day parts of the brush was worn away. Mary skillfully guided her horse to that spot in each jump allowing her mount to take each obstacle with just a long stride barely leaving the ground. It was a novice hurdle race for horses and riders that hadn't won a recognized race. Both Mary and her horse had obviously raced in quite a few unrecognized races. She stayed in the front increasing her lead after each well jumped hurdle and won by six lengths. I was impressed.

As Dan and I watched from our post the dollar signs were again flashing after the race as Mary had a hot walker and a groom for her horse who were being ordered around by an overly dressed couple who looked like the new money they were.

She was a plump women in her fifties, pale white skin, brown eyes, a large diamond ring on her left hand that sparkled in the sunlight, a large yellow floppy hat that covered most of her blond hair, a fur stole that covered the top part of some kind of fancy fuchsia dress and matching high heels that were getting stuck in the soft turf and he a tall slender man with mixed gray hair, ruddy complexion, ice blue eyes, wearing a dark blue business suit, blue oxford cloth shirt, a red tie and brogan shoes spit polished so his trousers that met the shoes at the instep reflected a mirror image. They were making sure everything was just right for their daughter.

Mary spotted me, waved, pointed me out to her parents, excused herself and walked over to where I was grazing Dan on a stretch of turf muddied brown from the cars and trucks. I told her I thought she rode well. She smiled the kind of smile that was cautious not knowing whether I was sincere or just being polite.

Dan had stopped grazing. He must have been getting tired of this socialite status. As Mary approached with an outstretched arm he lost his composure pinning his ears back and then attempted to turn his head to wheel and kick instead of accepting her pats. I pulled down on the leather shank attached to his halter tightening the chain across his nose and kept his head straight. He pulled against the chain and then wanted to lung at her, still keeping his ears pinned and would have bit her awaiting hand.

"What's wrong with him?" Mary asks with a puzzled look on her face.

"It's been a long day and he's getting tired," I said in a non-apologetic voice.

Reality Strikes My Dreams

I had hoped to be on the way home by now and this decision to watch her race has taken a lot out of both of us. It was time to get Dan on the van and start the long ride home. I was growing tired of being polite (I noticed her parents watching my every move) and began to walk Dan back. She trotted along to keep up as I heard her father calling her name.

The voice seemed closer and closer with each "Mary." She ask me for my phone number and as I began to give it to her I heard a gruff voice say, "That won't be necessary young man."

I looked over my shoulder and Mary's father was pulling her by the arm like a bad child back towards their waiting Mercedes. She again asked me, "What's your phone number?" As I told her I got a dirty look from her father.

Mary called me the following day. She came to the farm and I let her ride my other horse, one of the horses I told you my parents bred, that never came close to winning a race, Morning Girl.

But that's not reality.

Dan is mine, but Morning Girl is Steve's. We used to come over here together, especially for Sunday dinners, when he shared my apartment. My father liked him, so he came over with me often. Steve showed an interest in Morning Girl and my father gave her to him.

Dad figured out Steve and I weren't just roommates when he walked in the barn one Sunday afternoon. Steve and I were lying together on the cot in the tack room looking at a magazine of men's running clothes and talking about what we thought was under the spandex shorts. He told me later on he didn't like it, but accepted me for the way I was.

As I said before Steve only got kicked out after that first night in my mind. I gave him a second, third, forth, and so many chances I lost count 'cause I do love him. Not just the fantastic sex we had but he is really a nice guy and we had a really good thing going. I went to the racetrack everyday and he stayed home and kind of took over the role of the women in our life together outside of the bedroom (the roles switched back and forth in our bed). He used to cook our meals, do the grocery shopping, and even clean, sometimes. Anytime we went out people always liked him and treated us like we were a couple, even if they were sort of not comfortable with knowing two guys who fucked each other.

Reality Strikes My Dreams

When Steve and I talked it seemed like we were thinking the same thing a lot. I don't know how to describe love. I just know it felt good to have him around, except when he's drunk or high, the drugs are why he stole my camera.

We lived in this small town up north of the farm and you could walk everywhere to do your shopping and stuff. One day I came home from walking around and Steve was in my truck taking the radio out. He told me he needed some money to pay this guy who he got some stuff from. I didn't ask but I kind of knew what stuff he was talking about. I made him put the radio back. Later that night, after we had fucked for about two hours and I was asleep he came back down and took the radio. The next morning when he was gone I figured something was up, went down to the truck and saw the radio was missing. I made my mind up right then to put him out. This time he did leave. He's not here anymore physically but boy does that same mind that put him out that first night miss him.

When I told my father about Steve's stealing and that I had put him out, he still let him come to the farm, to ride and see his horse, but he was not allowed in the house like before.

Reality Strikes My Dreams

My father's policy didn't help me in letting go of my emotional attraction to Steve. Every time he would manage to get a ride to the farm, since I wouldn't bring him anymore, I would surrender to a compelling force inside my body that drew him to me like a magnet is drawn to steel. I would tell whoever brought him not to wait, that I would bring him back.

We would end up going riding and before we got back to the farm my hormones were raging just like the first time when I brought him home from the racetrack. I obeyed my father's policy, but as soon as the horses were cooled out I had my arm around him. Our lips would meet and we would make love out in the barn on that same cot my father saw us on.

Now that my father and mother don't live here anymore I am alone with my obsession toward Steve and it has been even harder to control. When he showed up this past summer, I still didn't let him into the house, but we had no trouble with our sexual exploits outside, since no one could see us. We'd lie nude on the grass and explore each other's sun drenched bodies the same way we did in the bedroom.

Why am I doing this? When my mind looks outside my body, it is very clear that a relationship with Steve is leading me down a toll road where the fees are more than I can pay. When I go inside my body, my thinking changes to a lonely man that wants very badly to have that warm body lying next to it in bed.

Shooting pain in my heart.

The first time Steve showed up, when Mary was here, he didn't like it that she was riding Morning Girl. Got a stare like what the hell was I doing with someone other than him, especially a woman? It kind of put me on the spot, because I hadn't ever told her the whole story. Had to do some fast explaining how this scruffy looking guy could own this horse and be a friend of mine.

See, Mary is not from the racetrack. She comes from an entirely different world, where her father is a doctor and they live in a well to do neighborhood. She has only gone to private schools and has never had any friends who are of a social status lower then hers, until she met me. Her father doesn't approve because I can't provide for her every wish. Sometimes I feel like a novelty Mary's using to go against her parents.

Ironically, Mary lives in the same neighborhood Chester came from. She remembers him getting into her family's garbage can and her father calling animal control. No wonder he has learned to maneuver his little body so quickly in all different directions. It was the only way he could avoid the loop pole the dogcatchers carry.

Mary's father bought her the horse she won that race on. Their trainer is the top trainer of steeplechase horses, whose farm is in The Valley north of here, where again; she doesn't have any contact with people of a lower social status then hers. So her reaction to Steve was not surprising.

Before these dealings with Steve, Mary had been to the farm several times, to see Dan, and go riding. Me on Dan, Mary on Morning Girl, and that's all that has ever happened. Mary is a good Catholic girl and proud of her virginity.

I remember the time we were taking a break sitting in a field of tall grass, tall enough to hide us from anyone who might pass by. Both horses were tied up to a near by tree. We started kissing and I thought of what I saw when she bent over in front of me that day at Dan's race. I put my hand under her blouse expecting to feel skin but was meet by a bra. She pulled herself away, and got up, her brown eyes shooting daggers. No words were spoken, but I knew from then on that the way she looked that day at Dan's race was just a come on and I was stuck at first base.

That's the way it still is, me playing the dangerous game of a love triangle. I question my sexuality sometimes. But how am I ever going to figure things out having relationships with a thief and a prude.

Reality strikes my dream.

The house is a large, two story colonial, constructed of clapboard, painted white with black shutters. Three, white, wooden columns, stretch across the front porch with the paint is pealing off of them as well as the clapboard and the shutters. The molding at the bottom of the columns is rotting away from lack of maintenance. A white, aluminum, storm door, covers a faded black paneled wooden door. A black cast iron eagle hangs over the door's white molded archway. My mother put it up when we first moved in. She loved eagles, and they are abundant in the decor of the house. Eagle light switch covers, hot plates, figurines, cross-stitch samplers, there everywhere you look. I put my key in the brass doorknob, open the door, and am welcomed by the pungent aroma of cigar smoke.

Reality Strikes My Dreams

Both of my parents are heavy smokers. It's gonna kill my mother, and my father's cigar smoking adds to his numerous health problems. The odor of his cigars still lingers throughout the house in all of the furniture and carpeting that they left here when they moved.

One thing I did get rid of was the fifth of bourbon that always sat on the kitchen counter.

My father's behavior, when he drinks, is determined by what's going on around him. I see it frequently at the racetrack. If his horse wins, he buys drinks for everyone involved with the horse's care. If the horse loses, he becomes enraged with loud words and actions. I remember, when Captain Jack lost a close race right at the wire, he kicked a chair in the box where we were sitting, sending it flying over to the next group of seats in the clubhouse. It almost struck the trainer of the horse who had just beaten us, a mild mannered man, who looked surprisingly at my father, wondering what to expect next. The security guards asked my father to leave. He did so cussing at everyone on his way out the door.

Reality Strikes My Dreams

My mother drinks too, but not like my father. She smokes cigarettes, one after the other. That habit annoyers me as much as my father's drinking. My mother always has a cigarette in her mouth and sometimes blows the smoke in many an unsuspecting persons face, which caused as many stares as my father's behavior does.

But the one thing about my mother that I found the most distasteful was her dislike for homosexuals. She despises them. She told me if I turned out like that she would lock me in a closet and through away the key.

My mother is sickly. I don't know for sure if she figured out that Steve and I were more than just roommates. But I think she did. She didn't seem to like seeing Steve and I together, and I was too old to lock in a closet, so she told my father to write me out of the will. I don't think he did since they are giving me the farm.

When I stop by to let her and my father know one of their horses is running she will greet me with a scowl. I know she is thinking, what are you doing here when I still want to lock you in the closet?

When ever I came here to visit the gripping talons of the eagle over the door used to haunt me. Inside I felt like the eagle light switch covers, figurines and cross-stitch samplers were keeping watch on the one they let get away. She'll never accept me and I know for sure that the eagles agree. But now I will have the final say when I throw all of the ones she left behind in the trash.

It's now 8:30pm and I haven't eaten dinner yet. Like to be in bed by ten, since I have to get up at four. Go into the kitchen, which is painted 1960's green below the white chair rail, and has green and yellow wallpaper above it. The white ceiling has a dingy, murky look, just as all of the ceilings throughout the house do, stained by all of the cigarettes and cigars smoked in here.

Opening the aged, copper colored, refrigerator the only thing I can find that is quick is frozen pizza, one of those small ones, supposed to be a single serving.

The directions on the package say not to preheat the oven. So I turn the oven on, and open the door by its chrome handle, put the pizza on the middle oven rack, and wind the dial of the yellow plastic timer that sits on the white marble like counter top, counter-clockwise, until the tip of the dial reaches 20 minutes, the time recommended. The appliances are all the original; copper colored ones, that came with the house, making them 20 years old. The aged oven takes awhile to get to the temperature needed and the pizza ends up taking more like 30 minutes. Sit down on a scuffed up wooden chair that along with three others, and a matching oval table complete the kitchen set that has been in this house since I was a child.

As I am eating, I open the mail. The first thing I open, is a stained off white envelope, with no return address. Thought it was junk mail, the same as everything else appeared to be. Put my finger into the open space on the top corner of the envelope flap. As I tear it open, a tattered piece of notebook paper, folded in three sections, drops out. I am stunned when I unfold the paper, and find a one hundred-dollar bill enclosed. On the crumpled paper Steve had written a note.

His handwriting looked more like scribbling, which along with, the wrinkled, grubby paper made his words difficult to read. I moved closer to the beams of the overhead light to be able to see what it says.

What I could make sense of at first was he thanked me for keeping his horse. The hundred dollars was to go towards what he owed me, and oh yeah he needed a place to stay, now that he had been ruled off the racetrack for stealing. Makes me wonder where the cash came from.

As I finish my pizza, I try to figure out what else he is saying. I was only able to make out several of the words: hustle, park, and 10pm. After several more attempts to figure it out I think I finally understand what his writing says. He has turned to hustling, he lives in the town park and if I can give him a place to stay I am to meet him there any evening at 10pm. Now I wonder if he stole the one hundred dollars, or it came from some trick he turned. There are a bunch of guys in town that would pay that much to get in bed with a young stud like him.

The faded old green wall phone rings, I never answer it this late, once, twice, three times, four times, and then five, before the answering machine picks up. "You have reached 765-9035, please leave a message," my voice says. The machine beeps and a static laden voice of Elvis Presley starts to sing Love Me Tender. That's the only words on the message, just the beginning of the song where Elvis sings love me tender.

Looking at the clock hanging on the wall over the kitchen door, it reads, 9:45. Steve. This is the type of thing he does. It's fifteen minutes before he hopes I will pick him up. Can see him standing in a phone booth, with that boyish grin on his face, tape recorder in one hand, holding it up to the receiver that he holds in his other hand, so I can hear his message. He'll quickly hang up the receiver if he hears me answer.

Shooting pain in my heart.

Can't be like the fly, the spider is anxiously waiting for in its web. Have got to escape the spider's tempting swagger and let him stay where he is.

The kitchen clock reads 10pm. Turn off the lights, and walk down the hall in the dark to my bedroom, get undressed and into bed. I lay there in the nude, remembering that this is the same double bed with its pink hand me down sheets Steve and I shared. My mother gave me the sheets along with the bed when I moved into my apartment. Little did she know the activities that would take place on her gift.

As much as I try not to, my inside thoughts of the passionate times we spent conquer my rational outside thoughts. The security light of the barn shines through the opening, where the two curtains don't quite meet. It cast a small ray of light across the bed, which reveals an image of swollen flesh my inside brain waves control. I think of Steve and me, our mouths and how he felt inside me. I moan and fall asleep with a warm feeling of inner peace, knowing that at least for tonight I have escaped the spider's web.

The phone's ringing wakes me up, the answering machine, my message and Elvis. I go back to sleep.

Chapter 4

Surprise, Surprise I hear Mick Jagger's lustful, clotted voice bellowing the opening line to the song of the same title, that he co-wrote with Keith Richards, as the clock radio awakens me. It's 4am. The lyrics go on to say, knew you was telling lies, knew you was telling lies, I could see it in you eyes. Wish I could play this back to Steve every time he calls with Elvis.

Reality Strikes My Dreams

Feel good about the decision I made last night and plan to continue to let Steve deal with the results of whatever he did. As I get dressed the lyrics of Surprise, Surprise keep on going around and around in my head, reminding me to allow my outer thoughts to take over the inner ones.

Put on the coffee and wander out to the barn, while it perks. Throw hay out in the field for Dan and Morning Girl. I hear them gallop up from the lower field, their hooves splashing in the water as they cross the stream. As they approach I see Chester scurrying along behind them. I pour his feed in a bowl by the fence. He waits for me to walk back to the house before he begins to eat.

The aroma of fresh brewed coffee greets me as I enter the house. The coffee is ready; I pour it into a travel mug, grab a bagel, go outside and start up the GMC, for the long ride to the track. It's now 4:30; I should get there by 6.

The vinyl seat is chilly on my legs and back on this brisk early fall morning. Take a sip of coffee to help warm me up, as I take the curve on the ramp and get on Route 95. Merge onto the highway behind a group of truckers and I feel drawn to become part of their convoy. My old truck is running good so I decide to stay with them as long as I can.

Their CB's tell them where the "bears" are hiding. Our speed approaches 80MPH, and the headlights of the approaching cars become dots of bright light flashing by. Ninety-five is lightly traveled this early in the morning; our group is able to continue its travel as one, our tires speed over the black asphalt that will take us where ever we are going.

My truck is shadowed by the big rigs and I can't see too much of what's in front of me. But I hear them down shift and by the approaching lights that reflect off of their polished trailers I know that we are approaching the tollbooths for the tunnel.

They all go to the right and use the lanes for the 18-wheelers. I bear left and use the booth for commuter tickets. Give the attendant the ticket, get the green light and pause after going by the erection and wait for the truckers.

As they shift their gears, gain speed, and enter the tunnel the noise in the tube rumbles off the tiled walls. The enclosure's lights become a blur as we travel. The first rays of sunlight greet us as we rise from that underwater container and begin to again get up to 80 MPH.

The convoy continues on its southbound path, and before long exit 10 comes into view. I leave with a flash of my headlights and a beep of my horn, wishing them a safe journey.

My mood is edgy during my brief ride to the stable gate. I'm relieved when I don't encounter Chubby as I enter, just the usual security guard, who examines my ID badge, comparing the picture to the face he is staring at, and he waves me on.

Dawn gives way to the brilliance of an early morning sun, as it rises above the barns and the backstretch yawns. I hear the rapid clapping sound of aluminum beating the asphalt, as a fractious horse makes its way to the track, its shoes doing a dance as its rider steers his mount in the correct direction.

Park my truck, go into the barn and am surprised that my horses are already eating. When I look to the corner of the barn, my eyes catch sight of the broken chains and the bent lids of metal cans, forced open to remove the contents. Oh shit, someone has stolen my feed. Just then Will appears around the corner. He sits calmly on his first mount of the morning. "I fed your horses, two quarts of oats apiece, I need to talk to you when I get back."

Watching Will walk his horse onto the asphalt path and then disappear, behind the barn next to me, I feel very lost, like a little kid on his first day of school, and the one friend he has made just left him alone.

Walk to the end of the barn, pick up the twisted lids and busted chains, and look inside, not too bad; looks like the thief only took enough to feed a couple of horses. Bend the lids enough, so they will rest on top of the cans, at least it will keep the flies out. Take the keys out of my pocket, unlock the locks, and throw the chains in the garbage, looks like they have been severed with a bolt cutter.

Turn around, walk back down the shed row to the first stall and start checking my horse's legs. Lucinda's Pet is finishing up the last of her breakfast, so I duck under the webbing before she starts her weaving. Her front legs are ice cold as I run my hand down from her knees to her ankles. She follows me to the front of the stall, and I as leave, she starts her dance weaving her shoulders right to left and stomping the opposite foot keeping time. "You'll be going to the track soon," I tell her, as if she could understand me. Her swaying continues.

Captain Jack stands at his stall door munching hay from the net as I unhook the webbing and go in. Stoop down on one knee and undo the safety pins that keep his bandages tight around his legs. His ankles are carrying some heat, but it's not too bad, since he just ran a week ago and he didn't get into the whirlpool yesterday because of the move.

After what has happened so far this morning I don't feel like dealing with Rude Awaking's antics. He is a pain in the ass and must know what I am thinking, as he stretches his head out of his tall door, and tries to bite me. He's never run fast enough to hurt himself. The only injuries he's ever had are from acting stupid. Take a quick glance at his legs as I walk by the stall. Looks like he made it through the night without doing any self-mutilation.

Will's figure comes into view from behind the neighboring barn. Anxiously waiting for him, to explain what happened, I can sense myself getting irritable, it's almost six-thirty and I haven't gotten a fucking thing done. Take off my cap, and use my shirtsleeve to wipe the sweat from my brow. Where the hell is he?

"I hope it was alright that I fed your horses," I hear Will say, as he walks around the corner.

"Yeah, but how did the cans get all busted up." I asked with a cross voice.

"Take it easy, I didn't do it and don't know who did. I told Mac about you and he said you could keep your oats and sweat feed in our feed room. Walk around the corner with me and I'll introduce you to him. , He's in there right now making up the hot mash for our horses,"

We enter a room on the south end of the barn, which is the same 10x10 size as the stalls. Its wooden walls have been white washed, and the dirt floor has been replaced by concrete, which has been freshly swept. A scraggly broom leans against the wall. The room is lit the same as the stalls, with a fly speckled bulb that hangs overhead. A middle-aged black man is stooped over a large steel container, stirring the contents with a long wooden stick. When he pulls the pole out of the soupy mush, I realize it is a piece of scrap wood that is carved to resemble a spoon.

"Mac this is Harry," Will says. As Mac turns and faces me, I notice he is a short man with a baggy tan cardigan sweater protecting a beige button down shirt. He wears brown cotton pants pulled up high above his waist trying to cover his pot belly, and white tennis shoes stained brown from their daily exposure to the elements of the racetrack. His weather beaten face encompasses brown eyes that have a gray blue tint. His friendly smile exposes his white teeth with gold caps on the front two.

Even though his face is wrinkled and shows the signs of his age I recognize it from pictures I have seen from a much earlier time in racing, when a number of the better jockeys were black. I remember what Mac stands for. Macabee Smith, one of the most celebrated jockeys in racing history.

But that's not reality.

Celebrated, in my mind and in those of his loyal, wealthy, owners, whose horses he rode, but not in the racing history books.

It was an honor to shake his hand. A hand that had experienced so much in what makes this industry what it is today. Maybe it would be different this time, and these two people would be the inspiration I needed to stop running from my fears.

"Very nice to meet you, Mac. Will speaks very highly of you," I say, as Will's face turns red.

"What you embarrassed about boy?" Mac says. "Nothing wrong with paying someone a compliment, you better get over that peer pressure shit. Just because the other guys in that damn bunkhouse think you're a wimp if you're nice to people, doesn't mean you need to act like them.

"Harry you can put your feed in this room. I lock it at night and I am always here by 5 in the morning, so it will be open when you need it. I need Will here in the morning. I got 30 head to go to the track. If you need him to work a horse maybe we can arrange something. We'll get along fine if you let him do his work in the mornings. What you two do after the track closes is none of my business."

Shooting pain in my heart.

What had Will told him? I just met him yesterday and Mac makes it sound like we are good friends and maybe even more.

"What you two do after the track closes is none of my business." Why would he say that? Maybe I am just too sensitive to what I think are sexual innuendos. Need to talk to Will, but Mac made it very clear, it HAD to be after he finished work.

It's now almost 7o'clock. I might as well move my feed, muck the stalls, and walk Captain Jack. Maybe a hot walker will come around the barn. That's how I got my first job. Just walked from barn to barn and asked if they needed help.

Finish mucking the stalls, no hot walker in sight. Walk Captain Jack and put him in the whirlpool. He'll stand in it all day as long as the hay net is full.

Getting Lucinda's Pet ready to go to the track, I get nervous about riding her, which is not good. A horse can tell how you are feeling just by the slightest change in your composure. She proves me right and ducks and wheels as I start our walk to the track.

It is a long complicated trip. The path weaves around the barn area finally ending up at a busy two-lane road with a crossing guard who stands in the street with a large stop sign, just like you were in elementary school.

An unsuspecting car screeches its brakes, as they approach, which scars the already fractious horses, including Lucinda's

Pet, who ducks away from the noise almost dumping me. Feel very self-conscious, thinking I should have been able to control her better. Don't know why, none of the other riders seem to pay any attention to me.

As we walk across the road and enter the racetrack Lucinda's Pet is her old self and tries to run off with me. Nothing doing, as I take a strong hold of the reins, arching her neck, and using every once of strength I have in my body to hold her to a slow gallop. After a quarter of a mile she starts to relax and I can ease up on my strong hold. The track is a mile in circumference and we travel the next ¾ without further incident. We get across the road with out a wait, which I am thankful for, and take the winding path through the stable area back to the barn. She galloped strong; see how she cools out, it might be about time to look for a race for her to run in.

After her bath, she gets Mac's attention when she bucks and plays walking around the shed, as she cools out.

"Is that the filly that just won last time she ran?" he asks.

"Yeah", I say timidly, not wanting to boast.

"I'd like to see Will ride her next time, talk to me about it later", he says as I walk past him.

"I need to see him ride a race, before I can put him on a horse in the afternoon." I tell Mac, on my next trip around the shed.

"Sounds fair, he's riding a horse for me in today's second race."

"OK, I'll be there", I say, anxious now to get my work finished.

Quickly I put Lucinda's Pet in her stall, hang her hay net and put the tack on Rude Awakening.

Rude Awaking snorts as he looks at his new surroundings, but remains calm on his way to the track as I talk to him quietly. Now knowing what to expect, I am surprised when we walk across the road again without a wait.

Rude Awakening is a large horse, standing 16.2 hands tall. A hand is 4 inches, so that makes him 5'6" at his withers; where the neck meets the back of a horse. He has a long stride, which eats up a mile easily, so I take him around again. It's the best he has ever galloped and I am pleased, as he is well mannered on our walk back to the barn. "Maybe you're finally getting the hang of this," I tell him, as I pat him on the neck.

Same routine as before, a bath and then walk 20 minutes to cool out. Walking past my stalls, I notice Captain Jack's hay net is almost empty. He will jump out of the whirlpool, knock it over and flood his stall, if I let him stand too long without something to eat. This is where the problems start when you're working by yourself and have two things to do at the same time. I quickly tie Rude Awaking up to the chain on the back wall of his stall, grab some hay and fill Captain Jack's hay net. Now he'll stay in the tub until I get finished. I untie Rude Awakening and finish our walk.

The track closes everyday at 10am. I congratulate my self on getting my horses out, even after the late start. As I turn the corner of the barn for the last time, I see Will rubbing Captain Jack on the head.

"You coming to watch me ride today?" Will asks.

"Wouldn't miss it. Going to get him out of the tub, feed them lunch, drive over watch your race, and come back and do their legs up. Be almost time to feed them dinner by then."

"Can I get ride with you? I don't have to be in the jocks' room until noon and it sounds like you'll be there by then," Will asks.

"Yeah I'd like that, but how are you going to get back here," I reply, hoping I could do that too.

"If you can wait ten minutes after the race I could catch a ride back with you."

"OK, I say. What did Mac mean when he said, "Anything we want to do after the track closes is none of his business?"

"I don't know. I just told him this morning how nice I thought you were. I don't have many friends around here, as you could tell by the jeers the other guys made yesterday, when I walked down to talk you. Mac has been a father figure to me, and as you heard this morning, he doesn't want me to be influenced by the other guys. Maybe deep down he believes as they do, that I am one of the faggots Chubby told you about. That's what I think he was talking about, the faggot thing."

"Is there any truth to that?" I ask.

"Well, maybe, but I don't want to talk about it right now, OK!"

"As I told you yesterday I am here any time you do."

He smiles and says, "I appreciate it."

Will disappears down the shed row as I get Captain Jack out of the whirlpool, dry his legs off, and fill his hay net again. "You're going to get fat old man, eating all this hay" I say to

Captain Jack, as he rubs his head against my back, his way of thanking me, for the additional portion.

As I turn around, Will is standing next to the stall with a bucket of oats mixed with sweat feed. "How much you feed them for lunch?" he asks.

"Two quarts mixed half and half just like you did, thanks!"

He gives each horse its ration as I finish cleaning up the shed row. We step into the GMC. I start her up and drive towards the stable gate. Chubby is standing outside and glares as we drive by.

"That man pisses me off, feel trouble coming on. Been dealing with people like him, questioning my sexuality, since I was younger than you. The time has finally come to stand up and fight."

"You serious? Will ask."

"Damn right, we need our own Stonewall right here."

"What's Stonewall?" he asks.

"It happened ten years ago, in New York City. Was a milestone in the fight for gay rights. Went on for four days at a gay bar named The Stonewall Inn. Police raided the bar, a commonplace occurrence back then, and the patrons fought back, just like we need to do. Chubby and his cronies are no different, this gay bashing has to come to an end."

"We need to talk more about this. I have known Chubby for awhile and you may not know what you're getting yourself into."

"Shit, Will you want to keep on going through what happened to you yesterday? What's it like in the jocks room? They tease you in there too? I don't know how old you are, but I've been teased since I was in junior high. The first time it happened I tried to fight the kid. He ran and got the teacher. I got scared and from then on either ran away, or ignored the pointing fingers and laughter. I have got to stand up for myself this time, not hide, letting Chubby crush my self worth along with yours."

Will put his hand on my thigh, "You're something else! You want to stand up for me too! Macs the only person who ever cared about me, but he couldn't help me with my sexuality. You know what I mean, never been there, so he just can't imagine fucking another guy."

Doesn't take us long to drive to the races. Entering the horseman's parking lot; Will pulls out his jockey's parking permit. The guard waves us on and we park on the front row.

Reality Strikes My Dreams

My old GMC looks out of place next to the flashy cars of the other riders. We show our badges at the entrance gate and walk in. Will heads off to the jock's room. "See you after the second" he says, with a smile.

Walk inside the grandstand, through its old wooden paneled doors with small window pains and peeling yellow paint. Buy a program, open it to the second race. Will is riding the horse trained by Mac. Opening odds in the program are 20-1, which means the track handicapper doesn't think much of the horse's chances to win. That can all change by race time. Could end up being the favorite, or the odds could go up even higher, depending on the amount of money bet on the horse.

The first race is on the track and warming up. Looks like a bad bunch of horses that have never won a race, called maidens. They are running for a $5000 claiming price in a race that is being run at 6 furlongs, which equals ¾ of a mile. I watch the race on the TV monitor without much interest.

Nervous and excited both, I wait for the second race to run. Since Mac ask me to watch Will ride, he must think his horse has a good chance of winning, no matter what the odds board reads. The big yellow numbers on the board flash as the money being bet is tabulated, 20-1is now 5-1. Good sign, other people are thinking the same as I am. The odds continue to fall and when the horses leave the paddock and enter the track, Will's horse is now the favorite at 2-1, as I bet $5 to win.

Push open the wooden paneled glass doors, with its peeling yellow paint, and walk down the slopping asphalt pavement, outside of the grandstand, to the fence which borders the track, and get a closer look, as the horses walk by in the post parade. Will is very serious, but manages to give me a sideways glance as he passes by.

Shooting pain in my heart.

My inside thoughts, hoping for a passionate event, combat the rational thoughts of my outside. My heart fluttered when he touched my thigh; you just met him yesterday. He told Mac how nice I was; you just met him yesterday. I like him a lot; you just met him yesterday. I bet he wants to go to bed with me; you just met him yesterday. The committee's conflict takes a recess. The horses are at the starting gate.

Reality Strikes My Dreams

This race is for maidens too, but of much better quality. They are also racing 6 furlongs. The bell rings as the doors of the starting gate swing open. Will's horse breaks with the others and is third, along the rail, two lengths from the lead, after the first quarter of a mile and they continue down the backstretch. As they approach the turn two other horses move up along side of Will. He is now trapped down on the rail, with two horses in front of him and the two along side blocking his path to improve his position. With the patience of a more experienced rider, he waits and then boldly makes his move through a narrow hole, next to the rail, when the two front horses drift out on the turn. As the field turns for home, Will is in front by a length. Now we see how he can finish on a horse. One of the horses that were on his outside, around the turn, rallies with a flourish. His jockey's frantically whipping him with strong right hand cracks, and his body's motion becomes one with the horse urging him forward. Will puts on an equally good performance, and his horse maintains a head advantage to the wire.

Won't be a ten-pound bug boy for long. My companion can, as a matter of fact, ride.

Will gallops his mount back to the winners circle where he is greeted by Mac and a very well dressed women in a business suit, shoes and hand bag to match. She is average build, about forty with long brown hair pulled back on a ponytail. She and Mac's faces beam with excitement as they reach up to shake Will's hand. They both stand at the head of the horse as the track photographer snaps the winner's circle picture. Will dismounts and weighs in. The track announcer voice comes over the public address system, "The second race is official and the winner was ridden by Will Carter for the first win of his career."

Mac and Will walk back to the jocks room along the outside fence of the track. The fans congratulate Will as he walks by. Anxious to see him myself I race to the paddock, so I can see Will before he goes into the jocks room. As he makes a right hand turn following the path from the track he sees me waiting. His eyes sparkle and his smile expands his lips to their maximum, becoming a toothy grin.

"Congratulations", I say.

"We are going to celebrate tonight. Just you and me, OK?" He replies, continuing to smile.

"All right by me," I exclaim, patting him on the backside as he walks away to change his clothes. He turns around and gives me that same smile as yesterday, when he looked at the front of my sweaty khakis.

When he walks in the jocks room two of his fellow riders douse him with buckets of cold water, an initiation of winning his first race. The track photographer walks out the door laughing, having just gotten a picture of the antics.

Walk back through the glass paneled door with the peeling yellow paint, up to the cashier's window, hand him my win ticket, and collect $15 for my $5 bet. Enough money to take Will out to dinner, maybe.

Time I get back to the paddock Will is waiting for me. "Where're you been," he asks?

"Just cashed my win ticket on your race, want to go out to dinner?"

"Yeah, sure," he replies!

"I am really proud of you. The way you ride."

"You serious, the part about being proud of me? No one has ever told me that before." He looks at me as if he is going to cry.

"Very serious, I won't bullshit you about anything. Just remember that!

" Let me tell you, I was worried about bringing my horses down here. You welcome me, made me feel at home, been my friend when I needed one the most, and I'll never forget it."

Will starts to cry as he gets into the truck, sliding over the bench seat to the middle, so he can place his left leg up against my right. I want to hug him and kiss the tears off of his cheeks, but instead I hand him my handkerchief.

"Thanks," he says.

Start up the GMC, back out of the space; drive out of the parking lot. Very emotional time, here I am with a guy I think I am falling in love with. He is crying because I expressed my feelings, and doesn't get angry but instead sits close to me. Our legs touch as if to show thoughts which we are both too shy to express and too scared, because of the surroundings we are in, to reveal.

Once we leave the parking lot, the roads are quiet, with only a few cars. Will again places his hand on my thigh, and rests his head on my shoulder. He has stopped crying and hands me back the handkerchief, which I stuff in the pocket of my shirt. His left leg begins to move up and down massaging my right. As I glance down to watch, I notice the bulge in the front of his pants. The sight of his erection arouses me too. Will's left hand moves from my thigh to the front of my pants. Taking my right hand off of the steering wheel, I place it on top of his bulge. Not speaking a word, we drive back to the barn.

Before we approach the stable gate, Will slides his hand off of my pants and mine slips off of his, as he moves over to the passenger's side of the bench seat.

"We are going to have our own Stonewall, sooner than anyone expects," I tell Will.

"Let's talk about it over dinner, he says.

"Can I go home with you? Mac told me if I won the race I could have tomorrow off. I can get my stuff together while you finish up with your horses. I can't stay around here. The guys in the bunkhouse, the same ones who torment me everyday, will want me to buy them some booze, and party. My own personal Stonewall starts tonight."

The GMC slows down as we make the left hand turn into the stable area. Chubby bounds out the guard's shack door and holds his grubby hand up for us to stop. Slithering, as a snake about to attack its prey, his beady little eyes glare at Will, as he approaches the passenger's side window. "Heard you won your race, you little faggot. What's wrong with jockeys now adays letting some asshole fucker win? Back in my time we'd have run you over the rail."

"You hateful bastard," I shout back, getting out of the truck I walk quickly to the other side. The rage inside explodes; my face is now so close to his that he can feel the breath of every word I speak. "Your twisted outlook on life has pulled me out of my shell, I'm fuckin' tired of this faggot shit out of your slack jaw mouth." Standing my ground I wait for Chubby to retaliate.

Warn holster shiny pistol.

He turns quickly, on the heel of his filthy brown work boots, walks back into his decrepit hovel, slamming the door. My heart's pound, pound, pound under my breastbone decreases. Rage is replaced with satisfaction of confronting this demon of my past that has humiliated me, crushing my spirits true feelings. This Stonewall had begun.

Will sits in the truck stunned by what just happened. His face is pale; his eyes have a vacant stare, as I drive back to the barn. He gets out of the truck and without a word walks to the bunkhouse.

Not sure what to say or do I walk into the barn. The horses are glad to see me. Can always depend on that. One of the things I love about this job. Can't go into an office and expect your co-workers to be glad to see you hundred percent of the time, like I can with mine. My horses are my true co-workers, not the people.

It's now 2:30pm, so there's an hour before feeding time. Have to groom the horses and do up their legs with any liniment and bandages they might need. Start with Rude Awakening. He requires the least amount of care. Brush him off, rub his front legs with alcohol, and put a set of bandages on them. Lucinda's Pet's legs are doing so well that she also gets the same treatment. Captain Jack demands a bit more. His old legs are still carrying some heat, even after the whirlpool. So a clay poultice is molded around his ankles and suspensories, wrapped in plastic to help draw out the warmth and then covered with bandages.

As I turn around and walk out of the stall Will is waiting for me.

"Can't believe what you did back there, you blow my mind. Needed to get my thoughts together that is why I left so quickly. Been an emotion filled day, won my first race, and became involved someone who understands me, all of me."

"I feel the same about you." I tell Will.

"Let's feed the horses and get out of here." I say, walking towards Mac's feed room.

Fill the three white plastic five gallon buckets with their rations, hand one to Will and carry the other two back up the shed row.

"They're all the same, just pick a horse and I'll do the other two." Will feeds Captain Jack.

Feel nervous, as I wonder if I will have to confront Chubby as we leave. Approaching the guard shack I see him standing at the door. He just stares as we drive past, what a relief, no more hostility, at least until tomorrow.

Just thought of this, Will has no idea where I live, must trust me. "Where do you want to go to dinner, I ask?"

"I really want to go to your place first, and then take it from there. By the way, where do you live?"

Smile comes to my face, "North of here, about an hours drive. I have a small farm I got from my parents. Have another two horses stabled there. Telling him about Diamond Dan and Morning Girl. Except for the fact that Morning Girl belongs to Steve. Too much information for now, he doesn't need to know about Steve or Mary yet.

As we approach the tunnel tollbooth I tell him about the erect penis, he laughs. Inside the tunnel we are the only vehicle. Will slides over, kisses me, and puts his hand on my crotch.

"What I told you about a rumor was a lie. The truth is Chubby caught me in bed with another guy when he was doing a surprise room check looking for drugs. Needed to get that out before we go any further."

"OK, I respect you for telling me," I say. Understanding all to well, how difficult it must have been for him to let me know. He slides back over to the passenger's side as we leave our short-lived privacy.

"There's some more I need to tell you," Will says nervously.

"Go ahead," I say. "I don't think there is too much I haven't heard before."

"When I was living in Florida things were a lot different. Most of the guys were rednecks like my grandfather. But then there were these other guys and those are the guys I got hooked up with."

Then he starts to tell me about his life when he was growing up and the "other guys". "I knew since I was about ten that I like looking at boys with their shirts off. My friends would be talking about girls and I wasn't interested. That was the first time someone called me a queer. I didn't know what that meant so I asked him. He said, 'You'd rather see me with no clothes on than any girl.' He was right."

"Sounds just like me," I said. Hoping to ease the edginess of the conversation.

Will looks over and smiles at me as he moves back over to the center of the bench seat and again he places left leg up against my right. He starts again his voice seemed a lot calmer. "The year before I went to the racetrack and met Mac I started going to the beach to get away from my grandfather. These other teenagers would be there practically nude with just a thong on. I'd get undressed down to my swimsuit and put my towel down on the sand near them and just watch."

"Must have been quite a sight." I could see his head moving up and down.

Reality Strikes My Dreams

"After awhile, like several days of me doing this, one of them came over and talked to me. His name was John. He seemed real nice and asked me my name and wanted to know where I lived and stuff, especially why I had been there several different times. I told him I liked watching him and his friends. When he asked me if I was queer I just said 'I don't know.'"

What happened then?" I was getting very interested.

"He asked me to come join them and I did. John and I started wrestling around on the sand and it felt so good to feel his naked skin against mine. Before long my cock was hard and so was his."

He stopped for a while and took a couple of deep breaths.

"Go ahead Will. It sounds pretty typical to me."

"Right behind where we were was a trail that went back into the dunes. No one is ever back there during the week so we got up and John led me by the hand down the trail. My cock was so hard I thought I was going to squirt any minute. But I was real nervous too. We only went far enough to be out of sight and John reached over and pulled my swimsuit down. I just froze as he got on his knees and sucked me off."

"Did you like it?"

"Yeah, a whole lot and I did the same to him. That was it my first gay sex. Really that was my first sex. I've never been with a girl. Have you?"

"Not really, just kissing and had my hand on this one girls blouse right on top of her boob."

"There is a lot more to the story," Will says as he continues. "So the next day I became one of the boys on the beach in a thong. I still didn't know what I was getting into. I asked John how come he was at the beach almost every day. Don't you have to work? He just smiled and asked me how old I was."

I knew then where he was going with this.

"I told him sixteen. He told me I looked older and he knew somebody who could make me up a fake ID. I asked him what for? He told me if I liked what we did yesterday I could make lots of money if I let somebody take movies of us doing it. But I had to be eighteen and that's what the fake ID was for.

"So that's what I did. At sixteen I was a porn star. I didn't know anything about saving money so I spent it all on anything I thought I wanted. I bought my grandfather a new television thinking that would stop the beatings. But he only wanted more and when I couldn't give it to him he beat me."

"Did your grandfather know where the money was coming from?"

"Yeah, he didn't care. Wanted me to do it everyday so I could buy him a new car; that's what the last fight we had was about.

"So that's what you're getting: A dropout, who's had more sex then most people twice his age, knows how to dance in the nude on top of a bar, how to use a gun and his way around in the bedroom but is lost anywhere else. You're the only person who knows all of this. I've only told Mac about my grandfather and being gay, that's it."

I took my right hand off the steering wheel and put it around Will's shoulders. He looks at me and starts to cry.

"I'm so glad I got all of that out," he sobbed and places his face on my lap. "How much longer before we get to your house?"

"We're almost there."

He looks up at me and says, "I've never met anybody like you before."

"I think you're kind a special too." We turn into the lane of my farm.

Chapter 5

Chester greets us as we turn into the lane. He can't keep up today as I drive quickly up the hill. He's just reaching the top when we are opening the front door of the house. "See you later buddy," I say closing the door. Will looks around the living room and puts his bag down on the padded armchair just inside the door. The pounding of my heart speeds up. I realize the things that happened in the truck were just the beginning. Here we are alone in my house and my shyness has taken my sexual desire hostage. I don't feel in control like I did with Steve: we had known each other for a while, had been flirting almost everyday and were both kinda inexperienced. Will's been around. I feel all nervous like I'm afraid I'll do the wrong thing. So just stand there staring at the floor..

Will puts his hand on my shoulder. I'm more comfortable and my sexual desire escapes. I raise my head. He looks me in the eyes and puts his lips against mine. I feel his tongue go in between my lips and press against my teeth. I open my mouth and our tongues move around each other in a circular motion. Their dance moves through out my body. Their energy grows and darts down my arms and legs and cock. My inner wishes are coming true.

I pull my lips away. "Come on with me." I walk quickly down the hall unbuttoning my oxford cloth shirt and unfasten my khakis. As I open the bedroom door my cloths fall to the floor and I drop back on to the bed with its pink flowered sheets exposing all God has given me. I watch Will strip. He struts over to the bed with moves of a bar top dancer showing off his body for tips. He leans forward and slides that smooth frame across mine until our bodies meet in perfect harmony to explore every area we can touch. Our sexual desires are released.

Reality strikes my dream.

Sleep comes quickly. The ringing of the phone interrupts our slumber. Still drowsy I let it ring four, five times and then Elvis sings.

"What the hell is that," Will exclaims.

"It's a long story that I can tell you over dinner."

It's now 7pm. Dan and Morning Girl pace the fence as a reminder it is past their dinnertime. Chester barks as he sees me looking out the window at them.

"Want to help me feed the horses and the dog before dinner?" I ask Will, putting only my boots on.

"You going like that?"

"Yeah, that something else I need to tell you. Around here you don't even need to wear a thong. We're secluded back here this far off the road. And there's woods all around the other sides. If you liked being nude then be that way. If not that's OK too. I'm nude whenever possible, which is most of the time. It's not just about sex like it was in Florida. My body just feels so good without clothes on it."

Will looks at me and smiles, "No wonder you didn't get upset when I told you about Florida. Yeah, I liked the being nude part the best. The sex with guys I didn't even know was hard. I had to fake it a bunch of the times."

Walking to the barn, our skins make contact again and the tollgates rise.

Shooting pain in my heart.

Dan, Morning Girl and Chester are now satisfied. I can't say the same for Will and I. As I bend over to clean up I feel Will's cock rubbing against my ass. I smile and lead him into the tack room. The cot awaits our bodies. Chester lies across the doorway as if to guard the two occupants against intruders. He is still there when we untangle our bodies and head to the house for dinner.

Will walks in front of me back up the hill. I enjoy the sight of his naked ass.

Reality strikes my dream.

I must pay attention to my feelings, the language of the soul. No matter how much I want to change my sexuality, I can't. I'm gay, not bisexual. Have to stop seeing Mary.

"Can we stay here and have dinner? Will ask. This nudity thing is cool. I'm not particular what we eat."

"How about subs? There's a shop up the road."

"Cheese steak with everything," he says.

I pick up the phone and order, "Two cheese steaks with everything, to go. Fifteen minutes. See you then."

Pull on a pair of shorts and a tee shirt and drive up the road and get our dinner. When I return Will is outside playing with Chester. I watch the motion of his exposed body parts as he runs across the lawn.

Shooting pain in my heart.

I notice he has poured two sodas, and has placed them on the white wrought iron table, with matching chairs, that sits behind the house.

Will takes the bag from me while I get undressed and join him for a dinner in the nude.

"Who was that on the phone?" Will asks. "You told me you would tell me about it over dinner."

"Oh yeah. His name is Steve and he used to work at the track as a hot walker, when I was still a groom. Was the first guy I ever lived with. We shared an apartment not far from here. Used to come home everyday from the track and fuck our brains out. It got old after awhile.

Came over here with me too and helped me take care of the horses. My father liked him. Gave him the filly out in the field for helping out. He still shows up here sometimes to see her."

"Were you lovers?" Will ask.

"Yeah. Don't worry. It's over. What's happened today between us makes me certain. What you told me about Florida doesn't make any difference in how I feel about you. What was it like doing porno?"

"It was fun at first and mostly with John. I'm not braggin' but after my first movie all the producers wanted me. That's when I started to hate it. I had to do it with some real sleazy guys. I had to fake likin' it almost every time."

"Why'd you learn how to shoot a gun?"

"That goes along with dancing on the bar. It didn't close until 2AM and by the time I left some of the guys I danced for would be really drunk and try to get me to go home with them. After this one big guy almost pulled me in the car with him I started packing a pistol. During the day I would go to the firing range and practice. I'm a pretty good shot. If this Stonewall thing gets out of hand I might end up using it."

"Well I hope it never gets that bad."

"Where is Steve now? Will ask. Why did he leave that message on the phone?"

"Got a note from him yesterday along with some money for the horse's care. He wants to come back and live with me. I won't let him. It's a fucked up situation. He's been playing that Elvis song on the answering machine, since yesterday.

"Plus he's homeless right now. Lives in the park not too far from here and hustles to get by since he got ruled off the track for stealing."

"And drugs," Will says. "I know Steve. He used to work for Mac. He was the guy I was in bed with when Chubby caught us. Steve had a couple of joints in his clothes along with a bit he stole off of one of Mac's bridles. Chubby had him ruled off. I guess you're the guy he told me he used to live with."

I didn't know what to say. I wondered now if I wasn't going from the frying pan into the fire. Will has really been around.

"What's wrong?" he asks.

"I don't know. You've just given me a lot to handle. I need some time to think all this through."

I get up from the table and take a walk down the hill towards the barn. Will never moves but I can feel him watching me. I didn't mind the porno thing but the gun bothers me. So does the fact that he slept with Steve and god only knows who else. No wonder the guys in the bunkhouse tease him, and then there's Chubby. I hear the sound of footsteps behind me. Will has run up to catch me.

"If you've changed your mind I can sleep out on the sofa tonight."

I look at him and shrug my shoulders. "Were you and Steve a regular thing?"

"Yeah, pretty much. I didn't do it with just anybody. I'd had enough of that. I can see what you liked so much in him and what you hated. He was really a nice guy inside. Just screwed up 'cause of his family and the drugs."

"He told you about his family?"

"Yeah, the redneck old man and the wicked step mother."

"That's them."

"You feeling any better about all of this?"

"A little. I just thought Steve was out of my life for good. Now I get a letter from him and am falling in love with his last boyfriend."

Will seemed kind of surprised. There was silence for a while and he just stared at me. "You know, no one has ever told me they loved me before. Or that they even thought they might. My parents both died in a car crash when I was three and my grandfather took over raising me, he sure never said that. I thought Steve might but he never did."

"Sounds familiar. About Steve I mean."

"As I told you before I have spent most of my life either with a grandfather who didn't want me, having sex or dancing nude on a bar. I don't know anything about life other than that. Do you get where I am coming from?"

"Yeah sort of. My parents never told me they loved me or taught me much about life either. They just bought me anything I wanted. Thought that was the way to show me they loved me I guess. So I don't know much about love either. I do know my insides feel different about you than any one else I have ever met and I hope that's what love is. The last two days have been incredible.

"Oh yeah, since we seem to be spilling our guts out there is one other thing I need to tell you, I have a girlfriend. Being with you made me realize what I really want in a relationship, and it not a women. I'm not going to see her any more. She's gone off to college anyway. Won't be back until Thanksgiving. Said she was going to write me. If she does, I'll tell her then."

"Is that the girl you felt up?"

"I wouldn't really call it that but she's who I was talking about before."

"I've never been with a girl. What's it like?"

"What we did today is way better. I am through being society's child."

Shooting pain in my heart.

When we get back up to the house I clean our sub wrappers and cups off the table and walk inside. I need to see what time it is. Will is directly behind me, and hugs me. I feel his body against my ass.

"You ready for bed?" I ask. "Four o'clock comes awful early."

Reality Strikes My Dreams

We lie naked, our bodies forming a perfect union on the sheets with the pink flowers. The phone rings five times, Elvis sings. Sleep prevails over any lingering sexual desires.

We are awakened by a clamor outside the bedroom window. The security light shines on Chester. He barks, growls, someone screams as his teeth pierce their flesh. Chester has the intruder by the leg and isn't letting go as much as his victim shakes him trying to pull away from the grasp.

"Fuckin' dog let go of me!"

"Need to break this up," I say, as I begin to walk out of the bedroom door.

"You're not gonna put any clothes on?" Will ask.

"I recognize that voice. Won't be the first time he saw me like this. You should come along and say hi to our buddy Steve."

"Oh shit!" Will exclaims.

Walking out the back door I yell "Chester." He releases his grasp. Steve holds his ankle and grimaces in pain.

"What the hell you doing here?" I shout.

"I need to see you. You wouldn't come to town and get me so I walked. My ankles messed up. I need to go to the hospital."

"Fuck you. You're lucky I don't have your dirty ass arrested for trespassing. Now get the hell out of here, now!"

"But I can't walk. Besides your standing here nude, sure you don't want some action?"

"Take him to the hospital, Harry." Will's voice says from behind us.

"Who's that?" Steve asks.

"Your savior."

"I wouldn't go that far," Will jokes. "Hi Steve."

Steve has a blank look on his face as Will walks towards him. "What the hell are you doing here? I heard you got suspended. But did they throw you out all together?"

"No, after Chubby found us fucking, asshole Ferguson gave me five days for suspicion of drugs and conduct unbecoming of a jockey. That was over last week and I won my first race earlier today. Chubby hates me even more now and I guess Albert Ferguson, Esq. will be watching me even closer every time I ride.

"But why are you here?"

Will couldn't avoid Steve's question any longer. "Harry and I are friends."

"In that case how about a threesome? I've been to bed with both you guys and it should be wild!" Steve starts to get undressed.

"No need to strip Steve. I like mine too much to put it near you anymore."

I nod my head. "I'll go along with that too."

Steve goes back to grasping his ankle, doing a lousy job of acting.

"Enough of the drama," I say. "I'll put some cloths on and take you to the hospital."

Will stays outside with Steve. Watching him I guess, even though Steve is probably doing some serious watching too. I hear Will tell him, "Harry told me all about you." I go inside to get dressed but I can still hear them talking through the open windows.

"Yeah, what'd he say? "

"How you lived with him for awhile. Now I know who the guy was you told me about. You're a dumb fucker you know it. You gave up an awful lot just to get high."

"My life's none of your business. You sure seemed to like fucking me. Didn't care about the drugs as long as we could get in bed. You're the dummy. Let me in your room with those joints just for a lay. Almost cost you your jock's license. You sure you don't want some for old-times sake?"

I came out of the house and Will was in Steve's face. "Get your dirty ass out of here before I give you a bite they won't be able to fix at the ER."

Steve gives Will one of those looks I know all so well. "You better watch him Will. He knows he can't fight but he'll plan some type of revenge, like the time he slashed my tires.

"Now get your horny ass in the truck," I say to Steve in an angry tone of voice.

Will looks at me and smiles as Steve limps over to the truck.

As we drive into town Steve puts his hand on the front of my pants. I push it away.

"Why'd you tell him about me slashing your tires?"

"I thought he should know how your mind works, if he doesn't already.

"Just remember Chester's always on guard. Next time you might not be so lucky."

We enter the circle in front of the hospital, by the emergency room.

"You need to get out. Don't come around at night anymore. "

"What's going on? We could have had a great threesome. You used to like to fuck all night."

"Got more than that now. I got love."

Shooting pain in my heart.

No answer from Steve. Didn't expect one. Never heard the word love when we were together. Elvis singing is the first time it has ever even been implied. He walks with a limp under the sign that reads EMERGENCY. The automatic doors open. He disappears.

Chester's eyes reflect my headlights when I turn into the lane. This time he is able to keep up and greets me as I get out of the truck. "You did good tonight little buddy, Thanks." I tell him as I walk towards the house.

Will sleeps on his back, across the contour sheet with pink flowers. It's too warm for any cover. The matching flat sheet is rumpled at the foot of the bed. The security light again shines through the crack where the curtains don't quite meet. It highlights his naked body.

Reality Strikes My Dreams

I undress and crawl into bed. He wakes and our arms wrap around the other's body, legs tangle, kisses are deep, until sleep conquers us.

Chapter 6

The alarm wakes us. It's 4am. I'm not ashamed of who's next to me in bed. No more Spider and the Fly.

"You staying here?" I ask Will. As I get up.

"Yeah, this is the first day off Mac has ever given me. It will be great to be away from the track for the day. I'll take care of things here. You'll be surprised. Ask Mac to introduce you to Cookie. He works for Mac and will feed for you tonight if you sit all the buckets out."

"Thanks, you want some coffee?" I ask.

"Yeah, never get a chance to drink any in the morning.

If you make a pot, I'll drink what ever you don't."

"What did you mean last night when you called Albert Ferguson, Esq. asshole Ferguson?"

"When Chubby caught me with Steve I had to go before the stewards. The other guys were going to let me off but Ferguson insisted that I get days. He told me that being in bed with another man was behavior unbecoming of a jockey. If I was caught again he would have me ruled off."

"That's just the kind of stuff Stonewall was about. I knew there was something about him I didn't like when he gave me the trainers test."

Try to get dressed while the coffee brews. Will still lies naked across the bed with pink flowered sheets. His body is calling mine. We become one.

Our union is far too short. I need to get to the track. I get up and put on my blue oxford cloth shirt, khaki pants, socks and brown paddock boots. My uniform. But I'm not hiding behind it anymore. I'm not the little kid in the hand me down Halloween costume. I'm proud of who I am. I like how I look. Pour my coffee and put on my British tweed cap.

"Hurry back," Will says.

I close the door and begin my journey.

My drive is typical as I join convoy of eighteen- wheelers. My speed quickens making the headlights blur. Think of Will when I see the erect penis. The noise vibrates in the tube. I travel south to my destination.

As I enter the stable area a guard checks my badge, no Chubby anywhere. I weave my way to the barn. The headlights of the old GMC reflect the shadows of horse and rider, on their way to the track. Approaching barn B the cast of their beam reveals the words fagot, homo, queer, written in black spray paint on my stall doors. The light extends just enough to expose a short stocky figure running away and tossing an empty paint can in the trash. The fight's not over, it's just begun. My own Stonewall must continue.

The adrenaline races through my body as I hurry to the feed room to get my horses breakfast. "Where's Will?" Mac shouts, as I enter.

"My house. Told me you gave him the day off. He wanted to spend it away from here."

Mac was so wound-up he had trouble getting the words of his next sentence out. "I-I-I-I did, but I was worried. Chubby's been here looking for you two. Said you faggots gotta go. What happened! What you boys do to deserve that?"

"I had a disagreement with Chubby yesterday. He stopped us when we came back from the races. Called Will a faggot and said the jockeys should have run him over the rail so he couldn't win. Pissed me off so much I called him a hateful bastard - that he had a twisted outlook on life and I was fuckin' tired of this faggot shit coming out of his slack jaw mouth. Now there's graffiti spray painted on my stall doors. Thought I saw Chubby's fat little ass running out of the shed row when I pulled up this morning."

"Sounds like he needs a visit. Feed you horses and come with me. It won't take long." Mac says, as he walks towards his car.

Quickly, I do as I'm told. Driving to the stable gate the intensity of Mac's emotions is very apparent on his face. He grits his teeth and those warm brown eyes are now glaring straight ahead. The skin on his face is drawn tightly, eliminating the wrinkles on his forehead and cheeks.

Pulling up to the gatehouse Mac slams on the brakes, intensifying the situation. Chubby, who is standing outside, turns abruptly and strides heatedly towards us. Before he can utter the first word, Mac jumps out of the car and is in Chubby's face heatedly expressing his dislike for the threat of yesterday.

"You fat little honky, want to see my boy get hurt. Anything happens to him and you'll wish you never opening that big mouth of yours. And I want all of that graffiti cleaned off Harry's stalls, now! You got ten minutes or I'm going to the racing commission and tell them about the police state you hold these men and women in around here."

Chubby glares at me, "I'm not done with you boy. You better bring Uncle Tom with you anywhere you go around here!"

Mac takes a step back and explodes with a left hook to the side of Chubby's face. Chubby's flabby jaw looks broken, as spit, which is now red with blood, spurts from his mouth. As he holds his jaw in agony Chubby motions to the security guard to grab hold of Mac, who now has his back turned, as he walks to the car.

"Watch your back!" I yell.

Mac turns quickly, pulling a switchblade from his pocket and activates its 6" blade. The security guard freezes in his tracks as Chubby falls to the asphalt with a thud and a groan; apparently, he's passed out from the loss of blood, which continues to pour from his mouth.

Warn holster shiny pistol.

"You gotta help him!" the guard shouts. He's still afraid to move, as Mac continues to point the knife at him.

"Get your skinny little ass in the guard shack and call 911," Mac orders to the guard, whose face is now extremely pale and body quivers as he walks to the office. Mac is close behind, his switchblade still drawn. But as they enter the guard picks up the police radio instead of the phone and screams, "Officer down".

"You underhanded bastard!" Mac yells. He slaps the young guard left-handed across his puny, pasty, white face. Still holding his weapon in his right.

Before Mac and I can decide what to do, three police cars and an ambulance arrive at the scene. They toss up gravel as they screech to a halt. The officers leap from their cars revolvers drawn. They look at Chubby lying on the asphalt, which is now a bright red as the blood continues to pour from his mouth. The paramedics kneel down over his body and place compresses in his mouth to stop the bleeding.

Seemingly unafraid, Mac steps out of the office door, leaving it open so the guard can hear what happens. The deputy sheriffs put their guns down as he speaks.

"Chubby threatened Will. Painted homophobic graffiti on Harry's stalls. And called me an Uncle Tom. Can't take a punch either," Mac says with a smirk.

Mac turns back around, steps in the office door.

"Don't forget, he tells the guard. You got ten minutes to get the graffiti off of this man's stall doors."

Dumbfounded, I shake my head as we drive back to the barn. Mac looks at me and says. "Just did what had to be done. I may not like to have sex with another man like you and Will but I won't let a man discriminate against another the way they did against me and my people for so long.

I train for some people who support my feelings and can shut this place down if they want to. Your stall doors are going to be cleaned off this morning, or Chubby and his buddies will be out of a job. Maybe that is what has to happen around here.

You and Will keep on fighting for what you believe in and I'll support both of you any way I can."

Reality strikes my dream.

"Did you know Albert Ferguson told Will he'll rule him off if he catches him in bed with another man again?"

"He did what?"

"That's what Will told me. When he went for his hearing the other stewards were going to let him off but Ferguson insisted he get days and told him then about not sleeping with another guy because it was behavior unbecoming of a jockey."

"Albert Ferguson, Esq. will hear from me later on this morning."

"Mac, thanks for all you have done for me. I know Will appreciates you. Thinks you are someone special. You know I recognized you the first day we met. Remember seeing you in a book at the library. Caption on it read Macabee Smith jockey."

"That was along time ago," Mac says as he shakes his head. You know I train for those same people who put me up on their horses back then."

"I know, Will told me the first day we met, made a point of it. By the way Will wants you introduce me to Cookie. Said he would feed my horses tonight if I put the buckets out."

"I'll send him around," Mac replies.

The rest of the morning is very uneventful. Except for watching that guard from the stable gate, who arrived a few minutes after Mac and I, scrub the spray paint off of my stalls. Sweat was rolling down his pale white face making dark black streaks as the dirt was stirred up from its crusted surroundings of the stall doors and settled on his skin. One by one the letters vanished as he scrubbed. Just like letters erased from a chalk board: F-a-g-g-o-t, a-g-g-o-t, g-g-o-t-, g-o-t, o-t, t- ; H-o-m-o, o-m-o, m-o, o- ; Q-u-e-e-r, u-e-e-r, e-e-r, e-r, r- . The hot walkers trudging by cooling out their horses made a contest of his labor. They counted how many more letters he had to remove. He was not amused but thought better than to say something in retaliation. Still, he grumbled under his breath, "Fuck you."

I found it amusing too and asked the hot walker who had just passed if they heard what he said. He hadn't. But on his next trip by he smacked the top of the guard's head with the end of the leather shank that held the horse at the other end.

Reality Strikes My Dreams

The guard stopped scrubbing the paint. Looked up at me glaring as if he was trying to project icy daggers out of his squinting eyes. Instead it just made his face scrunch up on the sides as he declared, "Fuck you too and your faggot jockey."

I smiled at his childish statement with a look of anticipated amusement; after all, Mac was walking around the corner and heard everything he said. With a hooking motion of his arms Mac picked the guard up by the back of his shirt collar, lifting his body off the ground. As he turned him toward the stall door he slammed his already limp body against the wooden barn.

"One... two... three..." counted the crowd of barn employees, who had gathered to watch as his face smashed into the barrier and blood ran from his nose and made a large irregular shaped splotch of red on the front of his white shirt. It mixed with the black sweat stains and formed a dirty brown pattern looking and smelling like a polluted stream. His screams became shriller each time his face met the wood. Until they gurgled as he swallowed some of the excretion and then silence when Mac let the body fall to the ground.

It lay in a heap. His arms and legs curled up under him and the shape of his torso resembled a pile of dirty cloths waiting to be washed.

He raised his head, looking over his right shoulder sheepishly. He cringed, expecting another blow, when he saw Mac was still standing over him.

"Get up out of the dirt boy," Mac barked. "The way I see it you still got five more letters to scrub off this wall and your times up. You're lucky I got too much work to do. But I got all these boys walking around the shed-row to keep an eye on you. Next time I come around this corner the marks better be gone along with you.

And Harry, I talked to Ferguson. He said that's the law. I told him he better be right because I was going to have one of my owners investigate it for me. He didn't know what to say then and hung up."

"OK, thanks."

I needed to be gone too just like the guard. It's now 7 AM. I feel alone... scared like the little boy away from home for the first time. Just as I thought I would until I met Will. My thoughts are racing like a runaway horse not knowing where it's going but running just as fast as it can to get there. I see Lucifer charging the webbing as a hot walker goes by, which stops the runaway thoughts like an outrider pulling up the horse before it can run too far. My horses need my attention.

Reality Strikes My Dreams

Reality strikes my dream.

The rest of the morning is pretty typical. Lucinda's Pet weaves and tries to run off with me on the track. Lucifer is a pain in the ass. Captain Jack is still sore and spends the morning in the whirlpool. My dynasty.

I bend under the webbing, not paying any attention when I leave Captain Jack's stall and bump into this large pair of legs. Looking up I see this round black man with a face to match grinning from ear to ear. "I'm Cookie," he says.

"Hey, it's nice to meet you. I recognize you from yesterday. You were holding the horse Will won on when they took the picture. I guess Mac sent you around?"

"Yeah, that's why I'm here watchin' you do up that old horse. You know I used to work for the guy you claimed him from. He thought you were crazy. Horse is ten years old, can hardly walk and some greenhorn trainer claims him from me. After you won a race with him the old fool stop bitchin', made him look like a damn fool. Anyway, he couldn't train a Billy goat to butt and Ol' Jack used to win in spite of it. How's the old guy doin' these days?" Cookie asks as he rubs the old horse's head.

"He's doing OK. I just love him, even though he's a lot of work with the whirlpool and everything. Always tries his hardest and that's all I can ask.

I'll have the feed sitting outside the door in those big white plastic buckets. If you can feed them around four that would be great. How much you charge?"

"Nothin'. Mac's takin' care of it.

"Something else, Will's been a friend of mine since he first showed up around here. I knows how he is and that you're fuckin' him. That's cool with me. Besides Mac seems to really like you and told me he'd pay me for helpin' you out."

The big smile on his face turns to a frown and he says in a serious tone. "You better take care of Will. You know he's like Mac's son and don't think he wouldn't whoop you like he did that guard this morning if you don't treat his boy right. I've said my piece..."

The smile returns to his face. "I'll feed them for you at night... tell that skinny ass jockey he'd better be here in the morning."

I watch his ass (it's big and round just like the rest of him) go down the shed toward Mac's feed room. Another angel to watch over me... I think my boyfriend has a lot to do with it.

Reality Strikes My Dreams

I remember hearing on the radio early one Sunday morning, "God don't like queers," from some radio evangelist as I drove to the racetrack.

People like Chubby think he right. Besides, it gives them an excuse for their gay bashing. But it seems like that preacher's story lands in the manure pit like all the shit around here with these angels my God has sent me. My idea of another Stonewall will need all of them to make it happen.

As I am leaving my main adversary stands at the stable gate... seems to be OK. I guess his jaw wasn't broken. Probably just knocked out a few teeth. He steps out in front of my truck, raises his left hand for me to stop and draws his pistol out of its holster with his right. I continue to drive directly towards him. Three feet, two feet, twelve inches... I'm so close I can see the broken button on the front of his dirty shirt. I glare straight ahead prepared to do whatever damage the front of this pickup can do to his fat gut. My right foot is firmly placed on the gas pedal. If he shoots the force of the glass breaking will throw me back and as I slide down in the seat my legs will be pushed forward and force my foot all the way down on the accelerator. My heart beats faster and faster as I await the crash. An instant before my truck's bumper touches his dirty khakis he quickly steps aside. He continues to point his gun at me as I drive by.

The ride home is a long one. There's a backup and the traffic is at a standstill, which stretches from the steel bridge where I am stopped all the way to the tunnel, which is about a half a mile away. As we move inch by inch it hits me, what happened at the stable gate. I could be dead right now. I start to cry and my tears mix with the sweat that rolls down my face. What have I gotten myself into? Will told me to be careful about confronting Chubby. But wait a minute; what am I thinking? I don't give a shit about Chubby and what he might do. I need to fight this time and stop the running; after all, he didn't shoot me! So I won. I won the first battle of this Stonewall! My tears stop and are replaced with a smile.

Reality strikes my dream

The little bit of air that was coming in the windows has stopped as we creep along making my clothes begin to stick to my skin. I unbutton my shirt, pull it out from the waistband of the khaki's and take my arms out of the sleeves, leaving the rest behind me to protect my skin from the vinyl seat. I leave my cap on. Taking it off would cause the sweat to run that much more down my face.

I undo the belt on my paints, unbutton the button holding the waist and pull down the fly. Whatever air there is feels good, one of the advantages of not wearing underpants. My body rises to the occasion.

A few minutes later the tollbooth's in sight. I cover myself as I drive past the teller and the erect penis. I think of Will. My foot presses down the accelerator.

Chapter 7

The grass shows signs of the heat, as it's brown on both sides of the asphalt lane of the farm. No people. No dog. No horses. They must all be trying to escape to sun's blaze. The horizon is bare except for a red Ford Mustang, parked in the turnaround spot at the end of the driveway. I'm not expecting any company. My pulse quickens as I pull my truck into the carport.

Reality Strikes My Dreams

You see it's only two steps from the truck door to the house and I hurriedly open the door not knowing what to expect. I hear groans then a scream from the bedroom. My pace picks up to a run as I plow through the kitchen and open the bedroom door.

I feel all of my self-control leave as I grab the naked body before it turns to face me. I have him by the throat and squeeze his neck so hard I can feel his pulse beating faster and faster then nothing as I drop him face down on the bed.

I know CPR and could revive the bastard. Instead I just hope he dies. Will lays face down, his upper-body strains to move with each breath. A bottle of baby lotion lays with the cap open on the bed. Will's ass-hole is still covered with the remains of the bottle's extraction. I turn him over and blood runs from his nose into his mouth. He coughs and coughs, trying to get his breath. The blood chokes him as I take the sheet to stop its flow. His breathing is muffled as he gasps for air. I put my fingers in his mouth. They slide over his tongue and curl up at the top of his airway sweeping away what blocks his breathing. He takes a deep breath, smiles at me and closes his eyes.

There's a pistol on the bed.

Reality Strikes My Dreams

The remains of what Will was choking on lies next to me on the pink flowered sheets, which are now blood stained turning the flowers brown, as if they had died. At first it seemed unrecognizable covered with chew marks and blood. Then the body I took for dead moved. He pulled his arms out from under him; one hand clenched the fingers of the other. That's when I noticed it. The top of his middle finger was missing and the joint hung open all of the flesh exposed. That's what I pulled from Will's throat, the fingertip of this guy who was raping him.

There's a pistol on the bed.

He began to scream as he held his mangled finger. I hadn't seen his face when I was choking him. I just wanted him dead. He lay on his side with his back towards me a familiar looking scar was just above the right side of his pelvis. And his ass I knew that ass. A bubble butt that I was only too familiar with. Steve. He turned to face me. His big dick flopped over his right thigh. It still has the extra large Trojan covering it.

There's a pistol on the bed.

"You bastard, you fuckin' bastard. I told you not to come around here. You're lucky Will was here or Chester would have nailed your ass good." My hand reaches the gun just before his.

His air passage is still recovering from my grip. He speaks in a weak, scratchy tone, "You son-of-a-bitch. Give me my gun."

"You wish!"

"Where's my finger? Where's my fuckin' finger."

I keep the gun pointed at him, reach to my right, grab his finger and throw it at him. It slapped up against his chest, Will's spit spraying out of it. He caught it before it fell to the bed and held it in his hand, examining it, trying to figure out how it would fit back on his hand. He started to cry.

"It won't fit, it won't fit. He bit off the end of my finger. I just wanted to fuck him again. He always did it to me. I just wanted to do it once."

The sobbing got louder as he repeated the phrase over and over, "I just wanted to fuck, I just wanted to fuck, I just wanted..."

He was interrupted by Will's screaming. He had regained enough of his facilities to experience the fire inside of his asshole. He sat up quickly, "Shut the fuck up," and nailed Steve with a vicious right hand. Steve lifted his good hand and began to sit up as the blood began to shoot from his nose. Will hit him again and again. I pulled Will away as Steve lie motionless on his back. The blood covered his chest as it barely moved up and down with each shallow breath.

I needed to do something, but what. Here I am in the bedroom holding a gun over two naked guys. One is still recovering from almost choking to death and the other, whose finger is bit off, is lying unconscious on the bed with his chest covered in blood.

I call 911 from the kitchen phone. Its cord stretches long enough that I can see into the bedroom. I explain to the dispatcher what has happened.

"I just got home from work and found this guy raping my roommate. When I pulled him off my roommate I notice that his hand was bleeding. My roommate was choking. I performed CPR on him and when I cleared his airway I removed the end of the other guys finger. While I was trying to help the guy with his finger my roommate sat up and cold-cocked him, a couple of times and knocked him out. I really need an ambulance."

There was nothing but silence on the other end of the phone. I imagined the dispatcher's face was white (things like this don't happen around here).

"Hello, hello did you hear me?"

"Yeah, they're coming," as the phone clicked dead.

As I walk back into the bedroom Steve has regained consciousness and is again holding his mangled finger. Will is lying on his back; his brow wrinkled and appears deep in thought.

"The ambulance is on its way, Will, please don't hit him anymore.

Steve gives me a little smile. I know that look all too well.

"I don't want you now or ever."

" Whose gun is this?" I say, waiving the pistol at them.

"Harry don't do that! It's loaded!" Will screams. "The pistol is mine. I told you I had it."

"I didn't know you meant with you."

"You should get some ice for his finger," Will says. "They might be able to attach it if you keep it cold." Will puts the gun back in his bag along side of the bed.

"You done fighting?" I ask. They both shake their heads up and down as I walk into the kitchen.

Before I can get the ice I hear the siren of the ambulance. I look out the kitchen door towards the living room window and can see it pull into the drive. A police car follows close behind. I greet the medics at the door. As I am showing them into the bedroom the front door slams and I hear the clipity clop of leather soles on the wood floor. They get less and less frequent as the strides become further apart in an attempt to catch up. A deputy sheriff joins us as we enter the bedroom.

Both Will and Steve lie naked across the bed. Will at the head and Steve at the foot, still holding the remains of his finger. The medics quickly attend to him and ask me to get some ice. When I return I hear the deputy say, "Can you cover up man," referring to Will.

Will sits up, pulls the end of sheet with the pink flowers over the front of him and says, "I don't want to press charges. Just get him out of here so I can rest and stop the pain in my ass."

"I've still got to ask a few questions." The officer says. How did this all happen? The dispatcher said someone was raped."

"I sure was," said Will. He held me down on the bed squirted that bottle of baby lotion on me and forced that big cock of his up my ass.

He had his hand right next to my mouth and I bit his finger. When he tried to pull it away I clamped down harder and bit the fingertip clean off. He stopped fucking me and grabbed my mouth and tried to get his finger out. He twisted my head around so much that I ended up swallowing. I was lying on my stomach trying to cough the thing up and he jumped on me again and fucked me some more. It hurt so much I was screaming and I guess I must have passed out.

That's when Harry showed up, after I passed out, 'cause he heard me scream. He must have got in here quick and pulled Steve, that's this guy's name, off of me. That's when I came to and was still choking and Harry put his hand in my mouth and pulled the finger out. When I got my breath I cold cocked Steve a couple of times and he passed out. That's when Harry called 911. That' it."

By that time the paramedics were ready to take Steve to the hospital. "Hey deputy we got to get this guy to the hospital. Can you talk to him there?"

"Yeah, I'll meet you there as soon as I ask these guys a couple more questions. "I still don't understand how this thing played out. Are these your clothes lying here on the bed?"

"Yeah," Will says

Reality Strikes My Dreams

The officer still looks puzzled as he ask, "They don't look ripped like he tore them off of you. How did you get naked?"

"You see," Will says. "I was already nude, outside playing with the dog. No one could see me. So I figured I wasn't doing any harm. Heard a car coming up the lane and I figured it was Harry. By the time I realized it wasn't I figured whoever it was had already seen me and it was too late to run into the house. So I just stood there with my hand covering me.

When I saw who it was I didn't know what to do at first 'cause he started taking his clothes off. Said he just wanted me to sit with him outside and surprise Harry when he got home. I knew Harry wouldn't be happy to see him here and I told him I thought he should leave. He was naked by then and was walking towards me holding his cock and asking me if I wanted any.

I know him all too well and what he wanted. I didn't want to fight so I started to walk away from him, down towards the barn, 'cause that's where the dog was. I knew Chester, that's the dog, hated him and would attack if I started to scream."

The deputy cut Will off and asked, "How did you end up in here?"

Will looked at him and rolled his eyes. "If you'd let me finish I'll get to that part. I couldn't find Chester so I ran as fast as I could into the house to get my gun."

The deputy stopped him again. "You have a gun? Where is it?" Will leans over and gets it out of his bag along with a piece of paper.

"Here's the gun and the license for it." The deputy examines both of them. He gives Will back the permit and keeps the gun.

"Why are you keeping my gun? I never shot it or hit him with it."

"Let me hear the rest of the story. If it sounds like you're telling the truth you'll get it back. If you lie to me you'll never see it again."

"Steve was right on my ass. I got the door to the house closed and wedged a chair in front of it. I ran in here to get the gun. But I guess I didn't do a very good job blocking the door 'cause Steve got it open and jumped on me as I leaned over to get the gun out of my bag. I managed to stick it under me so he couldn't get it. He wasn't strong enough to turn me over and I knew the safety was on so it wasn't going to blow my stomach apart.

That's when he grabbed the bottle of baby lotion off of the nightstand. I couldn't get him off of me and lie in the gun at the same time. The rest is what I already told you."

"How did the gun end up back in your bag?"

"Harry found it on the bed and gave it back to me."

"Is that right?" I shake my head yes.

"One more thing I got to ask. Are you queer or did he force his dick in you?"

"Whether I'm queer or not he raped me. I didn't want his dick stuck up my ass. Can I have my gun back?"

The deputy turns to me.

"How do you fit in to all of this?"

"I own this place and Will is my roommate." I didn't want to say lover yet until I knew Will really felt that way. Between being raped by Steve and what happened at the track this morning I've only been making problems worse for him.

Plus I don't know how the deputy would react. They're still kind of homophobic around here and me calling Will my lover would encourage him to fag bash, and I don't want that.

"OK for now. I'll need some ID from both of you," he says.

Will sits up trying to keep the sheet covering the front of him from falling off. When he reaches for his pants that are on the floor the sheet does not extend far enough and exposes his ass. It now has dried blood smeared over the pearly white skin of his butt crack.

When he sees the blood the deputy gets a shocked look on his face. "You sure you're alright? I see blood on your ass."

"I'll be OK." Will says, as he takes his badge from the racetrack out of his pants, which are now on the bed. I pull mine out of my shirt pocket.

"You guys both work at the race track?" the sheriff asked. As he looks at our picture ID's.

"Yeah, I'm a trainer and he's my jockey." I say.

Will gives me that sideways smile just like he did in the post parade.

"You guys win any races?"

The tone of he voice seemed more like what people have when they hope I'll give then a tip on one of my horses, rather then one of interest. "We're holding our own.

"By the way you better check out that red Mustang at the end of the driveway. It doesn't belong to either of us and if Steve drove it here it's probably stolen."

"OK. I will," and hands us back our badges.

"Don't you all go anywhere. I might need to talk to you some more."

He looks at Will, "You sure you don't want to press charges?"

"I'm sure," Will says as the deputy hands him his gun back and walks out the bedroom door. Clipity clop, clipity clop. The front door slams.

Chapter 8

I collapse on the bed, breathing a sigh of relief. Will's slides his naked body next to me. He feels warm as he rubs against my arm. He leans over kisses me and says,

"You saved my life. You saved my fuckin' life. You know that?"

I nodded. The reality of what I had just been through was beginning to sink in. I had no other reaction except to cry. I pick up the crumpled sheet with the pink flowers and wiped my eyes. I could smell Steve's dried up blood.

The smell reminds me of the time I told you about earlier when I helped Steve out. He was lying naked from the waist up on the dirt shed row, right in front of a stall that I was in grooming a horse. He had fallen when a horse he was supposed to be walking got spooked and ran off. As I said before the trainer he worked for was a drunk. It was late in the morning so he had been drinking for several hours. Was probably in a blackout and I'm sure he didn't realize what his employee was doing.

Steve was bleeding then too; only that time it was his nose. When the other hot walker he was working with saw him lying there and the blood she screamed and turned her horse around and started walking the wrong way down the shed.

The shed row is just like a one-way street. It only goes in a counter-clockwise direction. When she turned her horse around she was about to have a head on collision with the person behind her. Luckily he anticipated her u-turn and stopped far enough behind her that she and her horse were able to go the wrong way long enough to squeeze through the passageway in the middle of the barn. Where hay and straw are stacked against the walls.

Reality Strikes My Dreams

She put the horse she was walking back in its stall and returned in short order with a rub rag to put against Steve's nose to help stop the bleeding.

I had already pulled a handkerchief from my hip pocket. Put my arm around Steve and lifted him up from the ground to a sitting position. I had him hold the handkerchief against the end of his nose. It kept on bleeding and I was about to get him to lie down on his back again when his boss arrived.

He staggered while he stood there watching me. The aroma of cheap beer filled the air as it came out of every pore in his body. His breath smelled of stale tobacco juice, which he spit on the ground from the chaw in his right cheek. He slurred his words as he spoke to Steve in an angry tone.

"Get your skinny white ass off the ground and go down to my tack room. Don't lie here in front of this guy's stalls with that helpless look on your face you fuckin' fagot. This guys not going to suck your dick just because he's got his arm around your bony body."

I helped Steve up and as our hands touched he looked over at me with those bedroom blue eyes and I knew then I was had. Had to that slick come-on and when he did go home with me to the body that it came from.

"Sorry about all of this," the trainer said, as he threw me five bucks. "Get yourself a new handkerchief."

About an hour later Steve wandered back up to my part of the shed, after his boss had gone. As I said before he was naked to the waist and sat down on a bale of straw that was in front of one of the stall doors in that pose I described before. Feet flat on the ground; legs spread open, leaning back, his pelvis pushed upward. I was just finishing up feeding the horses lunch.

"Thanks for helping me... don't mind Joey, he's a drunk," Steve says.

"Yeah I know. How are you feeling?"

"My nose is sore.

"What Joey said about me is true. I am gay and I loved it when you put your arm around me. It's the first time since I've been on the racetrack that somebody was nice to me. Joey calls me faggot or queer about a hundred times a day. How come they don't pick on you?"

Shooting pain in my heart.

"They have before and still do sometimes. You just gotta get away from that drunk."

That's when my relationship with Steve really started. As I said before it has caused me a lot of problems; at any rate, what happened today was the worst.

Will begins to unbutton my shirt. It falls open as he undoes the snap on my khakis and pulls down the zipper. He begins to rub me ever so gently with his left hand until I am fully aroused. He slides down further on the bed until I can feel his lips and his teeth and his tongue. I turn on my side, open my mouth. My lips slide up and down, until the quake, the rush, the release. Some of it runs on to the sheets with the pink flowers adding another stain to mark the history of this day.

We move our bodies until our eyes meet Will smiles. "You ready for a shower?"

I start to shake my head in a positive fashion but stop.

"I need to tell you what happened at the track this morning."

I proceed to fill him in on the letters painted on my stalls, Mac's fight with Chubby, the antics of the stable gate guard and Chubby standing in front of my truck as I tried to leave.

Will just shakes his head and says, "All of that just because you stood up for me. I guess our Stonewall has really begun. "Let's get in the shower and we can talk about it some more."

The bedroom has two doors. The one that everyone has been using that leads from the side door of the house and takes you into the dining room, through the kitchen which has a door opening to the master bath and then into the bedroom. The other one opens onto the hall. The master bath doesn't have a tub or shower so we need to use the hall bathroom.

Before we can get off the bed the doorbell rings, then a knock and the side door to the house opens, clip pity clop, clip pity clop. The steps are heading towards the bedroom. We both freeze like deer caught in the headlights.

Reality strikes my dream.

"Looks like you're more than just roommates," the deputy says, as he stands in the bedroom doorway.

"I didn't mean to barge in but I've been ringing the doorbell and nobody answered."

"We've been busy," I say.

Just then Chester runs into the room and jumps on the bed.

"He belong to you? He ran in when I opened the door."

"That's the dog I was outside playing with when Steve pulled up." Will says.

"He belongs to us," I tell the officer.

"Can you guys get dressed so we can talk?"

"If you give us a minute we'll meet you in the kitchen. Right out that door," I say. Pointing to the door he came in. He turns around and goes towards the direction of the kitchen. I close the door behind him.

I turnaround and look at Will who is again lying on the sheet with the pink flowers that are now shaded with dark red and yellow.

"I don't want to answer and more questions; furthermore, I'm staying naked. This is your house and if you say being nude is OK than that's what I'm doing."

"I understand Will. Let me get a couple of towels out of the linen closet, which is just outside this other door. We'll have a toga party and wrap a towel around so it'll cover what he's so uncomfortable about.

"I'm glad you like being nude. It's a way of life, there is a lot more to it than just sex."

Will shakes his head. "I think I know what you mean. I had so much fun today being outside naked."

"Something else too Will, When we sit at the table I want to put my arm around you or at least hold your hand. This is a good chance to promote our gay rights here at home as well as the racetrack."

"Cool," is Will's response.

I open the door and we both walk towards the kitchen, our bare feet slapping the floor. Will's is wearing a dark blue beach towel with a white butterfly embroidered on it and mine is also a beach towel except it's got red, green and blue stripes. They cover our bodies from the waist down to our knees with the extra end flipped over our left shoulders. They slip and slide on our hips with each step, testing the tuck in the waist that keeps them from falling to the floor.

The officer seams taken back by our dress or lack there of. He sits on the far side of the rectangular kitchen table and faces us as we nonchalantly pull out our chairs. I sit in the one across the table and Will sits in the other perpendicular to where the deputy is sitting. He pulls the chairs out and turns it towards the deputy so he sits facing him. I slide my chair up so my stomach touches the edge of the tabletop, smile, and put my hands on Will's shoulders.

The deputy says, "This case is the first of its kind. We don't have any of your kind around here, at least until now."

I laugh. The deputy stairs at me with those dagger blue, how dare you laugh, eyes.

"Really, I say. I must be seeing ghost in the park. I guess it was my imagination when I got my dick sucked."

He sits up straight in the authoritarian cop posture, his right hand move to his waist.

Worn holster, shiny pistol.

He raises his left arm, straightens it out in front of Will's face, points his index finger at me and says, "Those guys aren't real faggots. They hustle any way they can to make a buck. I've hauled them in enough times I should know. Smelly, dirty asses in the back seat of my car."

"How do you know their not 'real faggots?" I ask. They've refused to suck your dick? You'd better be careful going into the park at night. Your big white ass would be fucked good."

He responds, " Anybody touches me and they'll be wearing the imprint of my billy-club."

"How long you been a cop?" Will asks.

"A year, and I've seen enough to know what I'm talking about." Thinking he has proved his point he continues. "I ask you guys to get dressed and you come out here just about naked. What is that you have on anyway?

"Togas."

"They look like dresses to me. All you faggots either don't want to wear clothes or dress up like women. I read it in the paper."

"What paper is that," I ask?

"The Inquiry," he says.

"Had a story the other day with pictures and all about how you guys love to be naked so you can do all that sick stuff you all do. And how one of you dresses like a woman so you all can try to fake a normal relationship."

I want to jump over the table at him but I thought better and said in an angry tone, "Get this straight. Us being naked has nothing to do with being gay. We like being nude. Being naked is a way of life. It has nothing do with our sexuality. And another thing we just put these togas on because you couldn't stand looking at us naked. This is my house and we should be able to live the way we want. You're luck we got dressed at all" I was wound up. "One more thing... I don't like the word faggot. We are gay!" By the look on his face I knew he didn't wasn't finish with us.

The arrogant tone in his voice continues. He looks at Will and says, "I just went to the hospital and Steve told me he wasn't raping you because you three are 'fuck buddies.'"

Will quickly gets up from his chair, grabs his towel at the waist pulling it off and stands over the deputy in a provocative pose. Like he was still a male stripper on the bar hovering over one of his bar stool patrons waiting for a tip. I know now why he started carrying a gun. With that pose he probably got more offers for a one-night stand than tips.

"Fuck buddies!" Looking down at his dick he says, "I like this too much to put it just anywhere." He spins around bends over and sticks his ass in the deputy's face. "See my red ass-hole? It doesn't get that way when you're buddies. He raped me. I told you. He held me down on the bed and stuck that big cock up my ass. That's why I bit him."

The deputy is ill at ease. He squirms and leans back in his chair. Trying to move as far away from Will's ass as he can. Still not satisfied with the distance he jumps up sending the chair over on it's back. His right hand moves to his hip. "He wants to press charges against you."

Warn holster, shiny pistol.

Will still has his back to the deputy and is clenching his fist in preparation to throw a punch. I leap from my seat and tackle him as the deputy is pulling his gun from the holster.

To make things worse the toga came loose from around my waist and it is still on the seat of the chair. My sudden movement had left it behind. I am now completely naked looking at the barrel of the deputy's gun. I feel like a robber whose mask had fallen from their face and they couldn't pull it back up and now are completely exposed.

Things are fucked up good! Will and I now lay naked together on the floor in a position as compromising as any we would have done in bed. My face covers his crotch like I've just performed some pornographic oral sex scene and this crazed cop stands over us with his gun drawn like he just broke up the filming.

He yells at us like a drill sergeant instructing new recruits. "You ass-holes! Get up off the floor and sit in those chairs." As we do he barks, "Pull them around, so you're both sitting at the table. "Slide them up and put your hands on the table where I can see them.

"What do you think we're going to do, I ask? We're nude. Where are we going to hide anything!"

He glares at me and says, "I'm getting sick of your smart ass remarks. Just put your hands on the table. I don't want you touching each other. It makes me sick."

We both put our hands on the table; meanwhile, I move my right foot over towards Will. I start to rub his foot with mine.

The deputy stands at his original place, leaning on the table. The gun lies along side of his right hand. He bends over towards us and says, "As soon as they release him from the hospital he's going to the station and press charges against both of you."

"When should that be? I ask."

"He might be there by now. They had finished sewing his finger back together and were getting ready to release him when I left."

His voice had quieted down and sounded more empathetic. "What happened here last night? You were talking about it before."

"He tried to break in this house and the dog bit him. Look at his right ankle. There are probably some stitches from when he went to the emergency room."

The officer had a puzzled look on his face.

"Let me explain," I said as he sits down in his chair. "Steve and I used to be lovers. I put him out when we were living in my apartment in Seaport. He stole from me. I pressed charges, look it up."

"What's his name again? I know its Steve but what the last name? Do you happen to know his birth date?"

"His last name is Burke. Steven Mark Burke. He was born May 14th 1960."

The officer gets up. "Don't move." I'm calling the station and run this through the data base." He says as he walks out the door.

I put my hand on Will's. "I'm sorry you have to go through all of this." I lean over and kiss him. His lips are warm and his kiss is full of unfinished business.

Clip pity clop, we part, our backs return to their full contact with the chair and our hands now only feel wood.

"You were right," he says, looking at us and checking out our posture. "He's got quite a record. Been in the detention center more than he's been out. Seems to be looking for three hots and a cot. I checked too and he hasn't pressed charges. I don't think they'd take him seriously if he did. Oh, and that Mustang out there belongs to a Patrick Burke."

"That's his brother." I say.

"Whoever it is they haven't reported it missing. Now that I got this information I don't have any more questions. You'll can get back to faggot fuckin'."

I didn't like what he just said but he was leaving and that was the most important thing. Will and I both stood up as he left so he got a full frontal nudity. He just shook his head, turned and clippity clop, clippity clop.

Reality Strikes My Dreams

Before he could get out the door Will was walking to the bathroom. Looking at me over his shoulder. Once the door closed and I knew the officer was gone I followed Will's lead towards the bathroom.

Will is waiting with anticipation. The warm water soaks our bodies before the soapy rub down whose aroma lingers as we dry each other off.

We spend the rest of the afternoon naked. Feeding the horses and us before our bodies nested on a clean set of sheets with the pink flowers.

Shooting pain in my heart.

Chapter 9

The radio plays our wake-up call. Paul sings, "Good morning, good morning." Our lips meet in passionate kisses like I have never experienced before. Deep French kisses have our tongues dancing and our bodies roll about the bed until the buzzer on the snooze alarm rings.

Reality Strikes My Dreams

As the coffee brews we enjoy the last few minutes of our nudity. The morning air caresses our bare bodies as we feed the horses.

"So Will, you liked being nude for the last day and a half?"

"Yeah, it was cool. I hate to see it end. Not like when I was in Florida. It was just a job then. I was glad when we stopped filming or the bar closed."

"I thought that deputy was going to shit his pants yesterday when you stuck your ass in his face. He was moving farther and farther away from you until he couldn't lean back in his chair and more or it would have flipped over."

"Too bad it didn't. You ever ride a horse nude?"

"Yeah, a couple of times. It's great! Next time you're here we'll go riding."

We go back into the house and get dressed. Clothes always feel strange on my body after being naked for so long. The coffee's ready and we're on our way. My thoughts change to Chubby and the racetrack. I wonder what I'll find there this morning.

Reality Strikes My Dreams

Will's leg touches mine on the vinyl seat of the old GMC. He snuggles close, putting his head on my shoulder as we drive the ninety minutes. When the rusty chain-link fence comes into sight he moves over to the passengers side. Chubby stands at the shabby screen door as we make the left turn into the stable area. My open window is beside him. He raises his right hand and waives us on, without speaking a word.

As we weave our way through the stable area the bright light of the rising sun flashes on and off as it peaks through in between the barns. At the end of the road, Barn B sits awaiting the morning activity, which, as we get closer, has already begun. Mac paces up and down the shed row in front of my stalls. Will and I sit up ready to springs from the truck as soon as it stops. I take but a few steps when I notice the three empty stalls. The white feed buckets I sat out for Cookie lie turned over in front of each stall, their contents thrown all over the dirt.

Mac meets us before we have gone but a few steps. "I'm sorry, I'm sorry, I don't know what happened. And Harry I didn't have your number. I got to have a phone number. When Cookie got here to feed your horses they were gone. The feed was like you see it. When I told Chubby he just laughed, like he was looking to get the rest of his teeth knocked out. I thought about it too.

"Plus, I couldn't get anybody but Cookie to help me look for your horses. Y'know how people be. 'Don't like faggots,' they said. The lady I train for showed up right after it happened. . She said the same thing. Chubby had stopped her at the gate and told her his version of what was going on. Whoa... it was the wrong thing to have happen. I tried to explain. She didn't want to listen and told me to take Will off of all her horses... and I was like no! I thought she was different. Y' know the world is crazy."

"Yeah," Will said, "and after I just won a race for her."

Mac's brow wrinkled as his eyes locked in on us. I felt shackled to the truck like a work release inmate.

"Whoa man, you guys are in some real trouble; but for now Will it's time for work. There's a horse tacked up and ready to go and Harry, you know there's a phone in my tack room and feed room, if you want to call the police or something."

Mac reaches out his right arm and the short sleeve of his yellow shirt recedes and exposes the well developed biceps covered with leathery brown skin as he puts that large weather-beaten hand on Will's shoulder pulling him towards the barn behind them and the waiting horse. He turns and his arm encircles Will's neck as he pulls him closer as a father would a child he is trying to protect from unfriendly surroundings.

Not a good sign I thought, jealously. There he goes with MY MAN. I could almost hear the fatherly advice taking him away from me. As they walked towards the barn I felt the chains that bound me to where I stood fall to the ground. I felt free to walk away from all of this. My horses are gone and I might have just lost the one person in my life that makes my head, my heart and the rest of me want to share all that they can offer.

It has only been a couple of days but I love Will. For the first time in my life I'm proud of being a queer. The gut wrenching gotta get out of here feeling I've had before is gone. I don't live with the ghost of my past when I hold his hand, feel his arm touching mine, his leg next to mine, or our lips meeting. You know what I mean.

I'm being pulled from both sides. Like the spoiled brat that I am, I want to get back in my truck, weave my way back through this dreary place and drive out that rusty old stable gate never to come back. But, as I look around at this environment I feel a connection to what surrounded Stonewall a few years ago.

Reality Strikes My Dreams

The Bowery bums were not much different than the hot walker who staggers down the dirt shed row. Walking a horse for two dollars and a promise of another bottle of Thunderbird. How much different is Chubby from the police who raided the Stonewall bar? He's following their example by persecuting us just like the police did the bar patrons because we are gay. It is time to fight back. Just like Stonewall this must become a milestone for gay rights.

I guess it's all up to me right now. I walk into the tack room at the end of the barn and stare at the phone hanging on the wall just inside the left hand side of the door. I hate using the telephone, guess it's because I stutter. The fact that I can't see the people on the other end that I am talking to makes me nervous and I hold my breath and no words will come out because there's no air to make the sound, least that's what the speech doctor told me when he made me practice breathing reciting the Gettysburg Address.

I pick up the phone "Four score and seven years ago..."

"County police."

I breathe. "I want to report a theft."

"What was stolen?"

"Horses."

"From where?"

"I'm a trainer. My horses are stabled here at Tri-State and when I got here this morning they were gone. They've been missing since yesterday afternoon according to the guy who feeds them for me. I just moved in here and he didn't have my phone number so he couldn't call me. That's why I'm calling you now."

I sighed a sense of relief that I had gotten through those four sentences without stuttering a single time.

"Did you tell Chubby about this?"

I knew I was in trouble when he called Chubby by name.

"Yeah, he was told about it yesterday. The guy who is stabled in the same barn as me, Macabee Smith told him and said Chubby just laughed."

There's snickering coming over the phone. "I'm laughing too because we don't help faggots." Then I hear a click.

"Hello, hello." No answer, he had hung up.

The only other choice I had was to call the man I'm scared of talking to the most, Nick Costello. Feel my chest tightening, "Four score and seven years ago..."

A voice answers, "Racing Secretary's office."

"Can I speak to Mr. Costello?"

"He's real busy right now, can I help you?"

It was J.P. The nervous guy who took me back to see Nick when I wanted stalls closer to home. I could imagine the anxious look in his eyes and the creases in his brow.

"Well maybe. Somebody stole my horses and the police down here refuse to help me. I guess if you ever want me to run my horses again you'd better help me find them."

I know I sounded smart-ass but I was proud of myself for saying what I said without stuttering.

His voice snapped, "Who is this?"

"Harry Brown," I said with as much intensity as I could. Knowing I could never match his. "I'm stabled in the same barn as Macabee Smith. One of his grooms was to feed my horses last night and they were gone when he got here. Mac told Chubby, the stable manager about it and Chubby just laughed. I just called the police but they hung up on me when I told the story about Chubby to them."

At first there was silence on the other end. Then he continues, "I've thought something like this might happen ever since you were here a couple days ago. Then when I saw you and Will together at the races I knew for sure. I guess you're finding out that Chubby don't like our kind."

I didn't know what to say. I guess that's why I thought he wasn't so bad after all when I left the racing secretary's office that day.

"Another thing, my father told me Mac had called questioning his decision on suspending Will."

"You're Albert Ferguson, Esq.'s. son?"

"You don't have to say all of that. Just call him Ferguson or ass-hole if you're pissed at him. I'll understand."

Then heard a sigh before he said, "Look Nick really is busy it's scratch time you know until 8. It would be best for you if Mac called Nick back around 9. After we get today's card settled, OK? Don't get me wrong it's not you. Its just Mac pulls a lot of weight around here. It would be better if he called."

Then I heard a gruff voice say, "Mac! What the hell's going on J.P.?"

"Gotta go, call back later." The phone goes dead.

I hang it up on the faded monkey shit brown wall and focus on the dust that covers it so thick you could write your name. I hope it will ring. But know it won't. I turn around. Mac's caramel eyes meet mine with a questioning look, as he stands behind the cooker, his arm muscles straining as he stirs the oats and sweat feed with a homemade wooden spoon, five strokes clockwise and the same amount counterclockwise. Much like he did the day I met him. I also notice another door on the back wall to my right. The way he must have come in.

I feel my chest tighten as I try to speak. I open my mouth move my tongue to form the word "I." But there is no air coming out. My mouth moves without making a sound. I stomp my foot trying to force the word to come out. I stomp and stomp my paddock boot on the concrete floor. The leather sole makes a slapping sound. Still no word comes out of my mouth. Mac stares at me puzzled look.

"What's wrong with you boy?"

I stop stomping, look at Mac and try again to say the word "I". My mouth opens and I move my jaw like I am gagging. Mac's eyes are so big that the whites show. He gets an alarmed look on his face like I am having a seizure or something. Abe Lincoln speaks "Four score and seven years ago..."

Air flows from my chest into my throat, "I stutter Mac. I was scared about what just happened on the phone. I can't get any words to come out when I feel so fuckin' afraid."

He again has that questioning look on his face, "What happened?"

The cops said, "We don't help fagots."

Mac shakes his head. The wooden spoon stops its circular motion as he let in drop to the side of the cooker. He turns to his left and walks out the door in the back of the room. I hear his car start as he revs the engine. Gravel hits a metal trashcan like bullets as he pulls away from in front of the barn. Kind of like a drag racer at the start of a quarter mile run. My stomach churns my heartbeat quickens. I turn around just in time and lunge out the feed room door into the shed row and puke on the dusty ground watching it randomly float on the dirt like oil on water. Will walks around the corner. His boots stop like they have been instantly concreted into the shed row. I heave again. Will's face is blurry. I grab hold of the wall. My legs feel like rubber bands. I feel myself falling as the dusty black wall phone rings.

Chapter 10

I awaken to the sound of sirens. Such a multitude of loud blasting noises that my mind goes into a flashback. To air raid drills in military school during the sixties. I stretch my arms up over my head and cover my face. Remembering crouching down in the boys locker-room, facing the gray metal lockers, naked, after athletics. Sitting on a wooden bench with varnish that made your wet ass slide off it.

Reality Strikes My Dreams

The wailing doesn't stop after sixty seconds like it did during the air-raid drill. My heart beats faster and I hear, "Harry, Harry," from a voice that sounds so familiar but is no one I remember from school. "Harry are you alright? Take your arms down, look at me."

I slowly open my fingers on the hand covering my face and I see the blue eyes, the shaggy blond hair, the weathered tan skin, the wet lips as the face gets closer and closer to mine. I start to cover up again, "It's Will, you're going to be alright. Take your arms down, give me your hand and let me help you up."

The sirens continue and I'm still not clear. I remember Robert Kohn. Him sitting next to me on the bench, as we faced the gray metal lockers. His naked foot rubbing against mine, his wet hip against mine and how our little dicks got hard.

I feel a thumb and a finger encircle my wrist on the hand that covers my face. I pull my hand closer to my face. But the grip around my wrist is strong. It pulls my hand away until my arm is parallel and lifts me to my feet. The left arm encircles my waist and yanks my body closer to theirs until the buttons on our shirt meet. I can feel the warmth and the tap, tap .tap of a heart beat and smell the scent of someone I know, I love. I feel my mind finally get things together. I turn my head towards theirs. He looks at me with a heart-melting stare. Our lips meet. As I feel a bulge growing in the front of my paints the sirens start again. I think of Robert Kohn.

I hug Will tighter and slide my right hand down from his waist towards his butt. It is stopped by something hard that is under his shirt, up against his skin and wedged inside the waist of his jeans. Will drops his arms away from my body, turns to his right and quickly walks away.

Before Will has gone too far two cops greet me. Who evidently are the results of the sirens I just heard. They must have been behind Will, when we hugged and kissed.

"Are you Harry Brown?"

I shake my head up and down.

"You're under arrest for the murder of Chubby O'Connor."

"What?"

"Anything you say could be used against you in a court of law..."

The one cop walks behind me, pulls my arms behind my back grabbing my wrist as I feel the metal band and hear the click.

"Will what the hell is going on?" I see his skinny ass plop itself down on the saddle of a waiting horse. They walk away.

"Will, Will." No answer as the horse and rider walk through the open door at the end of the barn, aluminum shoes click clack on the asphalt, the rider sits tight never looking back.

The cop behind me pushes me towards the waiting cruiser as the other pushes my head down as I climb into the back passenger side door. The cops get in the front doors of the car. The one on the passengers side in front of me turns his head around partway, glances back at me and says to the other, "Got to round these faggots up one by one like stray cattle."

The car meanders through the stable area and as we approach the stable gate we stop. I see a body on the asphalt covered by a sheet with a large red stain is on the front, about where the heart should be. The driver's side back door opens; a large body was thrust head first like a bag of laundry into the back seat. I recognize the yellow shirt. The officers again open both front doors and climb in the front seat of the cruiser.

Mac gives me a sideways glance and places his hands on his lap. No handcuffs. The fuckin' stupid cops forgot to put handcuffs on him. He reaches in the right front pocket of his tattered brown paints and shows me the nail. They must have forgot to frisk him too.

The wood on the barn is so weather-beaten that the old nails are always failing out. It's not unusual to have three or four old rusty nails in your pockets by the end of a morning. I guess this nail was one of those.

Regardless of where it came from, Mac uses it to jimmy open my cuffs as the police cruiser makes a left hand turn out of the stable gate and travels about a hundred yards until I hear the squeal of brakes and feel the sudden stop as my body is thrown forward, my face hits the back of the front seat and I can see out the front window of the police car. An almost white horse stands in the road and as I look up at the rider I meet Will's face. His eyes glare sharply as he fires a gun at the cruiser. The front glass shatters and at the same time the driver's cap flies off followed by a eruption of blood like I had never seen before. The cop's body becomes limp, hanging forward over his seat belt.

The other cop begins to turn toward Mac and me. I quickly stretch my arms out just in time to put my hands around his neck as he begins to raise his gun. Squeezing tight I hear him gasping for air as he struggles to break my hold. The adrenaline rushes through my body and I feel it strengthening my grip as I hear a crunching sound of the bones in his neck breaking. The officer's head becomes limp. I just killed a man! I let go of his neck looking at my hands. They are sweaty and shaking. How could I have done this, taken another human's life? Mac looks at me and sees my face.

"It's alright boy?"

I turn to answer him. "I----I----I---" Damn stuttering.

"You're white as a ghost." Mac says. "It was self defense. Any court of law will tell you that."

Mac and I jump out of the car open the front doors and pull the dead officers out letting their bodies fall to the asphalt. The events have drawn a crowd of horse and riders who are all lining up behind Will so many on each side until they have formed a "V' around the police car.

Will gives the sign. I start the car and follow him up onto the racetrack leaving the mob behind. We increase our speed as we begin to circle the oval. At the top of the stretch the grandstand becomes visible off to our right. As we approach I can see a figure standing by an open gate of the chain link fence that boarders the outside rail of the racetrack. They begin waiving their arms beckoning us to stop and come inside.

As we pass, Albert Ferguson, Esq. stands out on the track. He has walked away from the gate far enough that I can see him staring at me the same way he did that first time, when I walked into his office to take my trainer's test. He points at me shaking his hand as he screams at Will and I.

"You faggots are through!" That's all I could hear before we went past. But I could still see his mouth moving and his finger shaking when I looked in the rear view mirror. I imagine he ruled both of us off the track for good.

I continue following Will around the clubhouse turn on our way to the backstretch and where we had started. As we approached the opening where we came in a figure darts towards Will. The wrinkled brown suit gives him away: J.P. He takes hold of the bridle of the horse as Will comes to a stop and begins to walk beside him as we circle the track again.

"How did he get here so quick? How'd he know all this was going on? I just told him my horses were gone." I say, thinking of my phone call.

Mac looks at me kind of strange. "Boy you were out of it for at least an hour. Must've passed out right after I left." I shake my head up and down. "I heard Will call the stable gate right before Chubby and I got into it. He said you hit your head when you fell. Chubby called you both Uncle Tom loving faggots and that's when I pulled my knife. You would a been in the hospital by now if I hadn't stabbed him.

Then I remember about passing out and the lump I felt in Will's waistband. "I'm still confused Mac. Why did Will shoot the cop?"

"He tried to run Will over. Didn't you see that?" Mac glares at me like how could I have asked such a stupid question.

"I didn't see anything until I saw that white horse and Will aiming the gun. He told me he might use it if things got bad enough."

"You knew he had a gun?"

"Yeah, but I never thought he'd use it. We've been planning on standing up for ourselves and stopping the persecution, but nothing like this."

"Well you boys are in the fight of your lives right now. I'm willing to keep on fighting with you."

"Thank you Mac. Thank you a lot. I know now why Will thinks so much of you and I do too. You really think this was all in self defense?"

"I sure do! But that's not our worry right now. The cops will be here soon for sure. I want to get off this racetrack and stop just riding around and around."

Just then I can see in the rear view mirror that some riders are joining us, you know the ones who were forming the V around the police car and I notice one of the horses as it passes my window. It's got these big boned legs, not a racehorse, but some horse you'd see pulling a wagon. And the rider's legs seem like they're almost as big as the horses. Then I look up, Cookie, that round black face grinning from ear to ear. And what's that in his right hand? Looks like a couple long piece of wood with what looks like a torn up paper feed bag wrapped around the top of them. He kicks the horse in the side with the heel of his boot and they gallop up and walk alongside J.P.. Cookie leans over, says a few words and then hands J.P. one of the sticks. He then turns his horse to the left and as they walk away the feedbag unrolls. Painted on it in big black letters are GAY RIGHTS. When it finishes unrolling Cookie speaks to the crowd that has now assembled behind the car I am driving.

"This is why we're here. If you don't agree then get the fuck back to your barn."

As he glares at them a few turn their horses around and leave. Some of the others follow him and begin to line up on both sides of the car, protecting it like it had the president in it or something.

Cookie turns his horse around looping the sign in the opposite direction so that when he reaches J.P. and they change poles the sign is facing in the direction of the grandstand and Albert Ferguson, Esquire and a crowd of people who have joined him, as I hear sirens blaring and getting closer and closer.

I look in the rear view mirror expecting to see flashing lights at any moment. But wait! Am I seeing right? I motion to Mac to look behind him. He just shakes his head.

"You boys must have somebody watching out for you."

One of the track employees has closed the gates and taken a tractor and pulled the starting gate across the entrance. The sirens stop with a screech of brakes and loud screams.

"Police! Let us in."

When an officer tries to climb the fence the triple coil of barbed wire at the top puts his ascent to a stop. I'm sure one of them must have some bolt cutters and expect to see uniforms on the track very soon.

As we begin to approach the grandstand again Mac says, "You know that's his son."

Whose his son?"

"J.P. is Albert's son. He's one of you guys."

"Yeah, I just found out this morning when I was talking to him on the phone."

"I would have thought you already knew. But then again he's been hiding in the closet called the racing secretary's office for so long I guess you wouldn't know unless you were a trainer. I never thought daddy would ever let him out. I guess he finally decided to stop waiting."

As we round the turn, I can see the gate, the one that lets people on the track from the grandstand, open. Oh no, I guess the cops must have doubled back around the track to the front entrance. But wait that's no cop, its just Albert Ferguson, Esq. again and he got somebody with him. I can't believe my eyes. It's Nick Costello. Mac sees them to and tells me to stop the car. He winds down his window and yells, "Coming out." The horse and rider along side the car move over to let the door open.

I look again in the rear view mirror and this time it's not good news. I see the cops coming, guns drawn. More cops in one place then I have ever seen before. I guess they must have found a bolt cutter. Cookie has seen them too and motions to the riders. They move their horses right next to the car doors, trunk and as close to the hood as they can get without me hitting them. But it's not me they're after. They charge past the car and head straight for Will. He sees them coming and he and his mount quickly spring forward like they have just broken from the starting gate. Even the fastest cop is no match for them.

Albert Ferguson, Esq. sees them too, steps out to the middle of the track and raises his right hand. I wind down the window in the police car so I can hear what's happening. "Stop, put down your guns. This is Albert Ferguson, chief steward. I have everything under control." The cops slow down to a walk, guns still out of the holsters, ready for any chance to use them.

I hear Nick Costello tell Mac in that gruff voice, cigarette still hanging from the corner of his mouth his hand never touching it. "We found your boy's horses. They were up on the hill in that broken down barn no body uses. They seem to be all right. We put them back in his stalls."

"The guard at the gate told me he saw Chubby pull his knife first and you were just defending your self. But those two dead officers what are we going to do about them?" Albert Ferguson, Esq. ask Mac.

"Will shot the one because he was trying to run him over. It was as much self-defense as what I did. The other was ready to fire his gun at Harry and me when Harry grabbed him. The officer broke his own neck in struggling. That boy's not strong enough to break it on his own."

Albert Ferguson, Esq. raises his hand. His palm is facing Mac. "The coroner will have to determine that. Right now all three of you are still under arrest for murder in the first degree. But that's not all. Your owner said she changed her mind about your faggot boys. When she heard this story on the news, she went down to the court house and posted bail for all three of you." Albert Ferguson, Esq. shakes his head as if in disbelief. "You still need to go with the police and appear before the judge but you'll be able to leave afterwards."

The police are still standing behind Mac and in front of the car. Albert Ferguson, Esq. looks at them.

"I told you I had everything under control. I will have my chief of security bring them to the station."

The police turn and begin to walk back where they came from. As soon as he is sure they are leaving Will and his horse walk back and join the others.

Albert Ferguson, Esq. walks over to Will, Cookie and J.P. With a stern intense glare that again made the blood vessels on his face show he says to J.P., "I knew I couldn't keep you locked up forever, but this taking it too far."

J.P. looks at him, matching his facial expression but speaks in a calm clear voice; unlike the way he portrayed himself in the racing secretary's office. "It has only just begun," as a smile came over his face.

His father's mouth flew open as if he was going to speak but nothing came out. He just stood there with a stunned look on that ruddy face. His blue eyes looked weird like they became almost clear, kind'a blank. When he finally spoke his words came out slow and in a stern tone of voice. He paused after each phrase in an attempt to emphasize the importance of what he had just said.

"You... are NOT... my son any more. You are a disgrace... a disgrace to the Ferguson name." He paused for a bit and then started again, his voice was even harsher. "You are the first...

the first Ferguson not to go to law school. You wanted to work with HORSES. I got you that job in Nick's office. It was better than having you shoveling shit."

He got even louder... not talking real slow just loud. "Now you couldn't leave your cocksucker mind back in your bedroom. I don't want a faggot in my family. I'm done helping you out."

Then Mr. Albert Ferguson Esq. looked at me with a blank stair too. His face wasn't red anymore but kind'a white and with those clear eyes he looked almost dead. He walked over and shouted in the open window of the police car. But not the same kind of shouting he did at J.P.; instead, this was the kind of shouting Donald and Vicki did when they were calling me faggot.

"I KNEW THERE WAS SOMETHING DIFFERENT ABOUT YOU WHEN I GAVE YOU THE TRAINER'S TEST."

"What do you mean by that?" I said.

A smile came over his round face that made the red blood vessels surface again showing his true ruddy complexion. Those clear eyes started to turn blue again and had a look about them like I had asked the wrong question and better be ready to pay the consequences.

"I mean the way you walked and the way you talked I knew you were a fag, a smart fag but a fag. "

I pushed opened the door of the cop car, slamming it into Albert Ferguson, Esq.'s fat stomach. Knocking him backwards and off his feet. He fell on his big ass with his legs and feet sticking straight up in the air. I stood over him and looked him straight in those beady, blue eyes. "I thought you liked me after you announced I had won the first race I entered a horse in but it was just a bunch of bullshit you lying bastard."

He tried to get up to confront me but he was so fat he just wallowed around in the dirt like a pig ready for the slaughterhouse. He would get up on his hands and knees but when he tried to stand he would loose his balance and fall on his butt. He looked at me for help, then at J.P. and the others. No one moved until the third time he fell.

Nick Costello is puffing on that cigarette. That cigarette I told you before always hangs from the corner of his mouth. Puffing so hard that a cloud of smoke covers his face and also wraps itself around Albert Ferguson, Esq. When Nick helps him get to his feet he, Albert Ferguson, Esq., starts coughing and his breath blows the smoke away.

Albert Ferguson, Esq. gathers himself together and addresses the crowd. "As you all know I am the Chief Steward and I am giving you five minutes to go back to your barns or you will be subject to suspension and your licenses to work on the racetrack revoked."

He stands there with his hands on his hips and stares at this assembly of grooms, exercise riders, hot walkers, two trainers, a jockey and two racing officials. No one moves. His face gets that dead look on it again, until he looks like a large lawn ornament someone would have as a Halloween decoration to frighten trick or treaters. But it didn't work, because like our group, none of the kids were scared.

He doesn't know what to do; after all, he's an important person. Why weren't these people listening to him? He continues to stare at us. His head turns so his eyes can focus first to the group on the horses and those walking along side them, then to me and then to Will, Mac and J.P.

J. P. takes a few steps forward and spoke. "It's not going to work Dad. Your staring at us, it's not going to work. These are people; regardless of whether they are gay or straight they are human beings and deserve to be treated as such. Up until today this stable area was run as a police state. There were unauthorized searches of cars, stalls, tack rooms and even this man's (pointing to Will) dorm room."

His father was yelling again. "Chubby said he suspected drugs in all those searches."

"That's a lie. He suspected sex, gay sex and…"

Albert Ferguson, Esq. quickly cuts J.P. off. "That's even better. You perverts should all be stopped. Anal intercourse is illegal in this state. Chubby had the authority to arrest any one he caught doing such a thing. "

"But that's not the way it worked," Will said in an angry tone of voice as he moves his white horse directly in front of Albert Ferguson, Esq. . "He just stood there and looked at me and the other guy. Then he drew his gun and walked over so the gun was pointing right at my ass and made us do some more."

Will raises himself a bit from the saddle. He pulls the gun out that is wedged inside the waist of his jeans and under his shirt. He points it at Albert Ferguson, Esq. and walks his horse directly to Ferguson's right side. Albert Ferguson, Esq.'s face turns even whiter then it had before. His eyes look like they have fallen back into their sockets. I could see nothing but blacks spaces there, like a ghost mask is.

As Will gets closer and closer to Albert Ferguson Esq.'s face Ferguson's knees start to shake and he covers his face with his hands. "Take those hands away from your face and look at me. What's it feel like having a gun pointed at you? Are you scared? Are you," Will shouts? Albert Ferguson, Esq. shakes his head up and down. "Get down on your knees." Albert Ferguson, Esq. struggles and finally bends his knees and just falls to the track. "Now bend over and put your face in the dirt." Albert Ferguson Esq. hesitates until Will starts to pull the trigger back on the gun.

"Now I want the rest of you to leave. That includes you Harry and you Mac. All of you leave." Mac and I look at each other and then back at Will.

"Leave!"

"Will you're taking this too far. You heard what Ferguson said. Bail is already set for us and everything's been self-defense up until now."

"Leave Harry!" He takes the gun off of Ferguson and points it at me. "I'll shoot. Don't push me. You haven't been here that long. You don't know everything Chubby did with the permission of that ass-hole with his face in the dirt. I never told you but I over heard Chubby talking to him the other day. That's what did it. They had the whole thing planned. They hated us and were going to rule us off one by one. They got Steve. You or I were going to be next. I heard them talking. Now leave!"

The starting gate still blocks the entrance where we came in, so Mac and I get in the police car and drive back around the track following Nick Costello and J.P. as they walk together back to the grandstand. The rest of our troop has to do the same.

J.P. waits by the open gate for all of us to file out. As the last horse and rider leave he turns, pushes the gate closed and watches his father still kneeling face down in the dirt.

Then I hear him scream. "Will, don't." The sound of gunshots ring.

Reality strikes my dream.

Epilogue

Tri-State closed soon after and sits dark and empty. Recently there have been reports that in the last moments before sunrise a ghostly figure on a white horse has been seen galloping the wrong way around the racetrack. Something I needed to see for myself. Just like before, I leave my farm at 4:30 and drive past the rust chain link fence, as the sun is about to rise. When I make the turn to where the guy always stood with the stop sign I look to my right as the headlights cast their ray on the track and the ghost on the white horse goes past traveling the wrong way. I slam on the brakes and jump out to get a closer look but the track is empty.

Reality Strikes My Dreams

www.ingramcontent.com/pod-product-compliance
Lightning Source LLC
Chambersburg PA
CBHW031110260626
47172CB00001B/295